To Jane

Best

Catch 52:

An Everyman's Tale of Surviving in a Post-Brexit World

P G Ronane

Clink Street

London | New York

I would like to express my special appreciation to poet Kitty Kook for her permission to quote her poem *Soft or Hard?* in this book.

Published by Clink Street Publishing 2017

Copyright © 2017

First edition.

The author asserts the moral right under the Copyright, Designs and Patents Act 1988 to be identified as the author of this work.

ISBNs: 978-1-911525-80-6 paperback, 978-1-911525-81-3 ebook

For J. For everything.

'A man travels the world over in search of what he
needs and returns home to find it.'

George Moore

Chapter 1
Friday 24th June 2016. Morning

Deep inside he believed he knew the result and delayed switching on the radio, preferring instead to turn on the kettle to make coffee. He checked his watch – 04:56. Maybe, just maybe he had got things wrong. Perhaps during the night common sense had prevailed after all. He placed his cup of coffee on the kitchen table, opened the blinds to reveal bright sunshine, sat down and switched on the radio. The pips counted down to 5 am and the news began.

At 6:20 his thoughts were interrupted when Georgie, his 17-year-old daughter, walked into the kitchen. She ignored him, turned on the kettle and sat down at the table with her mobile phone. After staring at her phone briefly, she glanced at his untouched cup, 'Want another coffee, Dad?' After a short pause, he grunted, 'Got one thanks.' Georgie shook her head, got up, made two cups of coffee and took them upstairs.

He became aware of voices and movement from above, a toilet was flushed, followed by the sound of the family all walking down stairs together. They stood at the doorway of the kitchen. His wife Jane was the first to speak, 'Michael, I'm so sorry.' He knew things were serious when he heard the word Michael. Jane had not called him that for at least two years. Georgie, without taking her eyes from her mobile walked over to him, patted his head, picked up his cup saying, 'I think this requires more coffee.'

Jane turned up the volume on the radio whilst laying a hand on his shoulder. 'You were right about the result darling, even if it's not what you wanted.' Sam, their 14-year old son said yawning, 'You did say Leave would win Dad when the Sunderland result was announced.'

He kept quiet, not out of character for him. He nodded gently a couple of times responding to his son's comment. Meanwhile Jane and Georgie busied themselves around the kitchen preparing breakfast. The radio continued its non-stop commentary reaching the 6:30 headlines. The presenter announced the news to the Nation and the World.

'Britain has voted to leave the European Union...'

The silky voice of the BBC presenter spoke of areas that voted to Remain; London, Manchester, Leeds, Liverpool, Newcastle, Bristol, Scotland; then she started on the Leave areas. Wales, Birmingham, Sheffield, swathes of rural England and large chunks of the South, Midlands and the North, especially the run-down, former industrial towns.

Jane continued getting breakfast ready, occasionally helped by Georgie between glances at her phone. Sam had laid his phone on the table and sat listening to the radio with occasional glances at his father. The BBC were now talking about Sunderland as the early indicator of the eventual result and interviewing people in the city about why they had voted to leave. Most said immigration was the main factor yet a few did say that they felt that they had been cut off and forgotten by Westminster.

Georgie, still pacing about the kitchen eating toast, drinking coffee and picking up her phone, said in response to the radio report, 'Stupid Geordies, what do they know anyway? Even the football team's crap, although that centre-forward's dead fit.' Jane leaning on the work surface raised her eyes to the ceiling shaking her head at her daughter. Sam also shook his head, stating with some exasperation, 'First Georgie they are Mackems not Geordies, and their striker's Croatian, a long way from the north-east of England.'

'Mackems what the hell are they?' she asked loudly.

Jane said, 'All right you two, that's enough, sit down George and get breakfast.'

Everyone sat at the table, for Jane a welcome calmness came over her family as eating and drinking took the place of argument. After a few moments, Mike spoke for the first time, quietly and measured.

'You have to understand that many of the areas that voted to

Leave have serious social issues such as housing, unemployment, educational disadvantage, lack of investment, crime and racial and ethnic tensions. People in those places feel isolated and let down and this has been a protest vote by them. I hope that the government now realises it has to do something about this.'

Jane looked at Mike with a hope that his comments wouldn't start more family disagreement. Neither children said anything; Georgie and Sam were immersed in their phones, Mike drinking more coffee before announcing he was going for a shower. As he stood up Sam who had been typing into his phone said, 'It looks like the result will be 52 to 48 percent, Leave wins.'

He let the water cascade over his face and stayed much longer than his usual morning shower. What had gone wrong? The larger cities and conurbations with one or two exceptions, namely Birmingham, had voted to remain. University towns seemed to be strong remain supporters. The shires, suburbia, small town England, former heavy industrial areas and Wales all voted Leave. Scotland and Northern Ireland voted for Remain but what about Wales? What the hell was that all about? The Welsh had received more EU aid per head of population than any other part of the UK, what were they thinking of?

He had always found the shower a great place to think and this morning he needed to think. Perhaps there was a pattern emerging already about those who voted to stay or go. Probably an impossible task to sort out, the Leave voters seemed to range from the very wealthy to the very poor with everything in between. Likewise, the Remain camp. Perhaps education was the key, or age, race, class or culture, who knows?

What would they be thinking in the rest of Europe this morning as they woke up to the news? In Paris, there would be Gallic shrugs over their coffee and an acknowledgement that de Gaulle was right after all, the British would only wreck the project. What about Eastern Europe? The people who had thrown off Soviet oppression, hideous dictators and stagnant economies, they would not want to go backwards just as they were finding their feet. In Germany, the country that embraced the European ideal more than any other, there would be serious concerns about the potential economic consequences. They knew all about economic meltdown and what it led to in the 1920s and 30s.

'Dad, its 7:15.' Sam banging on the bathroom door brought him back to the fact that he had to get ready for work. As he dried off he realised that we must get on with this to the benefit of the country. The government would have its exit strategy in place and would swing into action without delay. Just as his own household had a set of unwritten rules and procedures each morning, the business of government would be clicking in with civil servants ringing their counterparts in Germany, France and Italy to book appointments for the prime minister to fly over and reassure the continent. Washington would also need a visit sooner rather than later.

As he came down the stairs the kids were about to leave for school, Sam in uniform, Georgie in her Sixth Form 'business attire' which was a cream blouse worn outside a short black skirt, black tights and flat shoes. Her hair had been piled up on top of her head which made her look taller and older. Mike disapproved but he wasn't sure why, perhaps he was just getting old. Jane was giving them a lift this morning and she appeared in the hallway pristine as ever in a black trouser suit.

When they had left, he relaxed and made himself another coffee. The radio speculated on what time this morning we would have a statement from Downing Street. The smart money was on sooner rather than later as the media was gathering in strength outside Number 10. This would be the statement to reassure the markets, allies and the British people that they had spoken and their wishes would be carried out, with the caveat that the responsibility was now with HM Government to sort things out and get us the best deal, which would most likely be a 'Norwegian' type of relationship with the EU. He had gambled and lost, he wouldn't be the first prime minister to do so, nor would he be the last. He would gloss it over with lots of 'I get it' and 'we go forward from here,' finishing off with a statesmanlike flourish that he had already been on the phone to Paris, Berlin and Rome, and would be on the plane over there early next week.

4

Mike looked at his watch – time to leave. He picked up his tatty canvas briefcase and walked out to his car. He looked like the many other male commuters leaving for work that day, blue shirt, sleeves rolled up, no tie, navy blue trousers and brown brogues. The sun was pleasantly warm and it was turning into one of those typical English summer days, not too hot, with the odd puffy white cloud in a deep blue sky, the sort of day that foreign tourists dreamed of as they booked their holidays here. He popped on his sunglasses, drove off the drive, out of his estate and onto the busy dual-carriageway that was one of the main routes into the inner-city. He decided he had had enough of news for now and changed stations. A Delius piece was playing, one of his pastoral English compositions, all sweeping strings and summer scenes, more than suitable. Delius, now there was a true English and European cosmopolitan if there was ever was one. Perhaps the producer of the programme was boxing clever on this historic day, playing an ultra-English piece of music by a man born in Bradford, of German parents, who travelled extensively and lived in France. This is what the English were all about, mixed, cosmopolitan, European and global. This was how Mike viewed himself.

Mike McCarthy was 58 years old and on a good day could look several years younger. He put this down to the fact that he still had a full head of mainly dark hair, had hardly put on weight since his early twenties and hadn't drank a drop of alcohol since travelling around Europe when he was young. This was tempered by the fact that he had smoked heavily until he was 26, when a bout of flu followed by pneumonia had put paid to his tobacco addiction. His relatively youngish looks were fortunate as his children were still young and his wife Jane was six years his junior. He was an art teacher at a large Secondary School in Liverpool where he had been for the past 15 years. In fact, apart from one or two early student jobs he had always been an art teacher, a career he loved, yet of late he had come to think of retirement more and more. Jane was the headteacher of a Primary School in south Liverpool where she had been since leaving university as a trainee teacher. Their children Georgina and Samuel were 17 and 14, respectively.

He parked the car in the packed school carpark and walked the short distance to a side entrance which was a short cut to the art department. As he walked through the door he glanced at the clock; just gone 8:15. He realised he had been up and about for several hours and was already feeling tired before the start of the school day. Angie Bell, the head of the art Department looked up from her desk in the tiny office they shared and gave him a nod, 'Morning Mike, bad result last night, that's democracy for you, give the masses the vote and look what happens.' Mike grinned going over to his desk to turn his computer on. He wasn't sure exactly which side of the fence Angie's Referendum vote fell on so he decided not to take the bait on this occasion. Kirsty, the department's current student teacher strolled in, eyes fixed on her phone. She stopped and her mouth fell open. After a short pause, she looked up and said without emotion, 'He's gone.' Mike and Angie looked at each other blankly before Angie said, 'Who's gone, where?' Another pause before Kirsty said, 'The prime minister, he's resigned.'

Immediately Mike put the news on his computer and switched on the speaker so all three could watch and listen. This was a whole different ball-game. Leaving was bad enough, but running away was a coward's way out, especially when you had called the referendum in the first place. If you make the mess, you clear it up, that had always been Mike's philosophy. The journalists were tapping their earphones and heading for their camera crews to comment as the famous door closed behind the prime minister. Mike became aware of someone sobbing behind him, looked around as Kirsty's tears spilt onto her phone. 'Jesus Mike, help her!' Angie called out as they both took an arm each helping her into a chair. Angie produced a tissue as Kirsty was saying, 'What's happening to my country, I've never known anything like this before, what's going on?' Angie was all reassurance, dabbing away tears, Mike holding her hand and telling her not to worry. Angie made her a cup of coffee and a smile came to Kirsty's face, 'I'm so sorry, it's just all this election thing, I'm just sick of the whole damn lot.' Mike and Angie smiled at each other as Mike said, 'Guess what, so am I.'

A few minutes later Kirsty was fine and busy laying out the

classroom as Mike and Angie looked on from the office. Angie sipped coffee and said, 'Do you know Mike, this referendum campaign has been the most divisive thing I can remember in this country. Thirty years I've been here and I can't recall anything like it… except perhaps when I was growing up in Derry, and that's not good.' Mike nodded and agreed that the level of debate had been abysmal with pathetic arguments, personal attacks, scare tactics and xenophobia bordering on racism at times. 'Well you know which side I'm on and ok, we lost, fair enough, I'm a good loser but I know that the over the next few days, weeks and months the issues will build up. This isn't going to go away.'

Angie thought about it before saying, 'Oh, I almost forgot, The Old Girl wants to see you at 9:15 this morning.'

He groaned, 'Oh, what the hell does she want now, if things aren't bad enough today!'

'Now that's no way to talk about our leader. She said something about the mock referendum the school held yesterday.'

'I emailed her the results last night, she obviously hasn't checked her inbox yet.'

'Well maybe she wants to make you the new departmental head of the politics class she's setting up for September. After all, you seem to be her pet man these days.' Angie smirked and winked.

'She can get lost on that one, I've got nearly double the amount of A Level students next year and anyway this school has never taught politics. We are currently five teachers down; the English department are down two.'

Angie shook her head and laughed. 'I'm only joking mate, don't take it to heart, but she does want to see you at 9:15. You're free first period.'

The bell rang and Kirsty was leading the kids into class as Angie put on her apron to take the first lesson of the day. He had 15 minutes to have another coffee and get his head together. He took a tie from his desk drawer – the head was a stickler for smartness outside of the art room.

The headteacher was Rachel Evans. She was one of those women whose age was difficult to assess. She looked anything between 35 and 45, depending on what she was wearing. Her nickname 'The Old Girl' was simply because she was a former student of the school and it had been with her since she had first arrived four years ago as headteacher. Recently, some of the younger teachers, especially the women had started calling her the 'Sixth-Former'. Mike had asked Angie what it was all about and she told him that they thought she dressed too young for her age and wanted to look like the Sixth Form girls. They both agreed that this was juvenile, but laughed anyway.

Several weeks ago, Rachel had stopped him in the corridor and asked could she have a word? She told him 'We should do something in school about the forthcoming referendum.' She went on to say that she felt he was the 'right man for the job as he was very politically astute.' Mike wondered why she should think this but listened to what she had to say. She told him that she wanted him to organise a debate in the school about the Referendum. He could invite the public as the audience and she handed him a piece of paper with three names and contact details of expert panellists. Another name at the bottom he recognised as a local radio presenter who had volunteered to be the debate adjudicator.

One thing that Mike admired Rachel Evans for was her use of the media. On her very first day as headteacher, the chairman of the Governors had introduced her to a packed school hall as 'our very own Rachel' and she had spent the next hour giving interviews to television and radio stations about how much of an honour it was to 'come back home' and the 'importance of continuity.' She was certainly shrewd in this area and it proved useful for the school in lots of ways. If a pupil had achieved something special she would see to it that it was on the front pages of the local paper and there would usually be a feature on one of the local radio stations. If the local or regional media wanted a comment from a headteacher about the latest proposals from the Department of Education, then guess who would pop-up that evening on TV? Her greatest coup came three years ago, when she had sent a memo to all staff to tidy up their departments and themselves for a 'special visitor' the following day.

As everyone arrived the next morning they found the carpark

full of vehicles from TV companies and camera crews setting up all around the school. The pupils were convinced that the queen herself would be arriving in no time at all. Angie had been informed that her department would be visited by the guest and she and Mike spent the first hour tidying up and pinning up the better pieces of art. He just had time to put on a tie and jacket before heading over to the window to look across the carpark to where Rachel and her senior staff were waiting outside the main entrance. There was no sign of anyone else. The bell rang and a few moments later a few A Level students wandered in for their lesson, followed by Stefan Zelenski, an out of breath member of the Leadership Team. 'Angie, Mike, he's here, and you're first on the list to be visited, get these settled down quickly and start your lesson.' Mike told the boys and girls that they would be visited in a few minutes' time by a guest and the lesson would carry on as normal. As he finished speaking Rachel walked through the door followed by an entourage of dark-suited young men and women, some carrying notebooks. Rachel and the others looked back to the doorway where Her Majesty's Secretary of State for Education was giving high-fives to two Year 8 pupils who happened to be passing. He strode in and introduced himself to Mike, Angie and the students, told Rachel that he would like to sit in on some of the lesson, removed his suit jacket and sat on a vacant stool between two students. The young men and women from the Ministry gathered around opening their notebooks as Mike began, 'OK everyone, this morning we'll be considering Andy Warhol's contribution to the Pop art movement of the 1960s.' The Secretary of State beamed, looked around at the students and said, 'Fantastic.'

He received a brisk 'Come in' to his knock. 'Hello Michael, hope you are well... What do you think about the result?'

'Which one?' he said with a smile.

Rachel looked at him quizzingly, her head leaning to one side before she smiled, nodded and said, 'Ah, very good, ok, let's do it chronologically, firstly, the school Referendum yesterday.'

Mike sighed before saying, 'The result was 60–40 in favour to

Remain which was a big majority. Surprised me a bit, thought it would have been closer. Perhaps it's indicative of how young people think or maybe it's just a reflection of how their parents voted, after all, the city voted to remain.

She said, 'I think I know what you think about the other result. It was close though.'

'Which will only cause more problems as a we go along with each side claiming a victory of sorts. The Leavers will be saying we should be getting on with it while the other side will say there is no clear mandate for change. I can see this going on and on.'

'Michael, I want to thank you for all the work you've done on the Referendum and especially the debate. I had lots of messages from parents saying how interesting and informative it was.' She stood up, picked up a piece of paper from her desk and walked around to him.

'Guy Simpson, you remember him hosting the debate? He's holding a two-hour programme this lunchtime about the Referendum. He wants you to take part. Don't worry, I see you haven't any classes this afternoon. Here's his number, give him a call and see what he wants... You know I would normally do this sort of thing myself but as I told him, I know just the man for the job.'

Before he could object she was tapping his arm and ushering him out of the door saying, 'Thank you so much, I know you will do a smashing job on behalf of the school.'

He looked back at the door as he walked down the corridor. Yes, the Sixth-Former's skirt was too short and her blouse too tight.

As he sat down at his desk he received a text message from Jane.

Hi Mike, don't forget, we are going out with Tim & Sinead tonight. XXX J.

He replied, *Yeah, no problem. M.*

He looked at the piece of paper with Guy Simpson's phone number. Simpson was one of Rachel Evans' smarmy, jumped-up radio and TV journalists who swanned around her like vultures looking for a story. Mike suspected there may be something more going on between this vulture and the Sixth-Former and if so, he simply didn't care.

The school Referendum debate had been held three weeks ago, during the evening. Simpson had waltzed in to the event in a packed school hall like he owned the place. Something of a local celebrity, straight away he stood out from the crowd. Whilst Mike and the rest of the panellists were dressed smartly in suits, Guy Simpson wore a pair of skinny fit jeans, tatty moccasins, a pink polo shirt and an old leather bomber jacket. He looked like a 40-year-old teenager and had the place in the palm of his hand. He stood at the front of the stage and spoke for ten minutes to the audience. Starting off by thanking Rachel Evans for inviting him, he told the audience that they were privileged to be a part of an historic debate in what was possibly the most important vote they may ever cast. He said that he wanted to hear some common sense and realism from the panel on the stage behind him because there was little on display from senior politicians up and down the country. He told them he would be inviting questions and comment from them throughout the evening. He mounted the stage to wholesome applause, led by Ms R Evans, Headteacher.

Mike had agreed with Rachel beforehand that he would be on the Remain side yet would be apolitical, taking a neutral view. He was on the panel with a young man from the Greens whose name was Connor and had stood unsuccessfully on two occasions for the local council. He believed firmly in the principle of the European Union. On the Leave side was a middle-aged member of the Labour Party, Jack Nelson, a trade unionist and a local councillor. The fourth member of the panel was a member of UKIP who had previously stood as a parliamentary candidate in one of the Lancashire mill towns. Between the two sides in a central position sat Guy Simpson.

Mike knew that Simpson would have done his homework where possible on all the panellists. There was a fair bit about the UKIP man on the internet as he had fought a Westminster by-election. The Labour man, Nelson had a colourful history having been a member of the Militant Tendency during the 1980s before returning to Labour in the mid-1990s. He had popped up in books, magazines and television documentaries, and was well known in the local area. He was an experienced and aggressive politician. The Green candidate was barely 23 years old, seemed rather shy and was relatively unknown to the public. However, Mike McCarthy knew he was a talented debater, politically astute and nobody's fool; he was a former pupil at the school and one of Mike's old art students.

Each panellist introduced themselves and gave brief reasons why they supported one side or the other. Guy Simpson then asked questions that had been submitted by the audience as they entered the hall. Mike took a low-key stance on why we should remain in the EU, citing the official line of stronger, safer and more secure in, rather than out. The UKIP and Labour representatives answered in the opposite way, with few policy differences, stating that Europe was run by bankers and bureaucrats who didn't have Britain's interests at heart. They both mentioned the fact that they wanted their country back but differed about immigration. Connor spoke about damage to the environment, the economy and life chances of young people should we vote to leave. The whole thing was going along fine and Mike could see a beaming Rachel in the front row.

During the interval drinks were served in the adjacent school canteen with Rachel making straight for Simpson through the crowd. Connor was in the middle of a bunch of young people, some of them current students of the school. The UKIP man stood amongst a group of people who were probably family and friends, whilst the Labour councillor sat amongst a mixed group which consisted of a couple of school governors, staff and local people. Mike stood in a corner with a paper cup of tea nodding to a few of the students and their parents. He felt a tap on his arm, looked around and saw his daughter Georgie.

'I didn't see you in the hall, I didn't know you were coming.'

'I'm sitting near the back, well done Dad, you're doing really great.'

'I'm not doing much at all if the truth be known, I'm surprised people haven't dropped off to sleep.'

Georgie laughed and looked about. She saw someone and

gestured to them to come over. A girl about Georgie's age and a boy walked over, drinks in hand.

'Dad, this is Amy and Matt.' Mike presumed they were from Georgie's school, although they looked older. Whenever he bumped into his own students out of school they always looked a few years older.

He said, 'What do you think of the show so far...? Sure you want to stay for the second half?' They both smiled, nodded and said 'Yes' together.

Georgie said that Matt was quite political and had been out campaigning for the Remain side in his spare time. Mike, intrigued asked him what he had been doing.

'Oh, just setting up a trestle table with a few others, wearing those blue tee-shirts, giving out leaflets and so on.'

'In the city centre?'

'Yep, along Bold Street and in Uni.'

'You're a student at the university?'

'Third year veterinary.'

'OK, I see... Are there any other students here apart from you?'

'About fifteen of us tonight, we try to get along to most of the local Referendum events.'

Mike looked about for the girls but they had wandered off, talking to some others. More university students? Georgie caught his eye and smiled encouragingly.

'And does Georgie help you lot out with your campaigning?'

Matt smiled, shook his head and said, 'You know Georgie, Mr McCarthy, she's totally not political, doesn't even get involved in our debates. Too interested in her art and poetry. Nice to meet you anyway.' He walked away to join the others.

Mike thought to himself. At least fifteen university students in the audience on the Remain side, which could be useful during the second half and one of them appeared to know his daughter well.

Guy Simpson started the second half of the debate with one word, 'immigration'. After two written questions and answers from the panel he invited further questions from the public. A middle-aged woman stood up and said,

'We need to stop messing about and stop people coming into this country, what do this lot think of that?'

There were rumblings and one shout of 'Shut Up' from amongst the audience. Mike looked at Rachel sitting in the front row who was looking worried. Guy Simpson paused before inviting Mike to speak first. Mike looked directly at the woman who asked the question as he answered.

'First I want to make it clear that this debate is about whether we should stay in the European Union, or not. It's not directly about immigration, however, I'm presuming the lady who asked the question is referring to immigration from the EU so I will deal with that... Two weeks ago, I visited my mother who was in hospital. The doctor who was treating her was from Germany, the practice nurse on duty, from Spain, the ward orderly from Ireland and the cleaner from Romania. Now all these countries are members of the EU and certainly that day and probably most days whilst she was there people from the EU looked after her... And it's not just the National Health Service who require immigration from the EU, our financial services, our manufacturing base, our service industries, agriculture, higher education and thousands of other jobs are dependent on workers from the European Union.'

He paused for a moment before raising his voice and saying, 'If we pull out, so do they and the inevitable consequence will be the collapse of our economy.'

There was much applause, particularly from the back of the hall where he could just make out Georgie and her friends on their feet, clapping. Rachel was smiling and applauding. There were a few shouts of 'What about the English?' and 'Send them home.'

He took a drink of water and knew what was coming from Guy Simpson.

'Thank you, Mike, but people do have concerns about immigration from the EU and aren't all these people taking jobs from people in this country. After all, what about the effect on our infrastructure, schools, hospitals and so on?' Applause for Simpson, mainly from the side of the hall where most of the Leave supporters seemed to be sitting. Guy gestured for Mike to answer.

'We mustn't forget that it's not all one-way traffic. There are an estimated one and half million British people living and working in the European Union, many in top jobs in the scientific community, education, IT industries and finance, but others in catering, entertainment, music, tourism and care jobs. Perhaps the biggest group of all are retired people soaking up the sun in Spain, Portugal, France, Italy and Greece; they impact on those countries services and infrastructure… Not on ours.'

More applause, again Georgie's student group were on their feet, some clapping with raised hands. More shouts from the Leave side, 'Answer the question!', 'English jobs for English people.' Mike also heard what sounded like 'Fucking teachers' from the same area. Rachel must have heard this as she looked back, scanning the hall for the offender. Simpson had his hands raised, palms up, calling for quiet. As the noise subsided he said with a broad smile, 'Good! Things are heating up, let's continue!'

Looking back Mike felt that the school debate had gone well. He looked at Guy Simpson's phone number, checked the clock, 9:40. He had twenty minutes before his class. He picked up the receiver.

Chapter 2
Friday 24th June 2016. Afternoon

He drove along the dual carriageway that was known by just about everyone as the 'Dock Road' towards the taller buildings in the centre of the city. He checked the car's clock: 11:50. The midday light blazed through the windscreen as he put down the sun visor. Simpson had seemed rushed and impatient over the phone but surprisingly grateful that Mike was coming to his show. The event was being held at a large exhibition centre overlooking the waterfront which was part of the city's urban renaissance over the past 15 years, much of it paid for by European money he reflected.

As he approached the centre he saw thousands of people coming and going along the pavements and crossing the road towards the river. Amongst the office workers there were the large groups of tourists who seemed to have flooded the city of late, filling out the hotels and boosting the local economy. Tourists would have been unthinkable back in the 1980s when this road was a windswept wasteland of bomb sites and boarded-up buildings and the only migration around was away from the city, as fast as the nearest train, boat or plane could take you.

He parked in a swish underground carpark and headed towards the river. As he approached the exhibition centre he could see a queue of people being marshalled by young people wearing tee shirts with the centre logo. He wondered just how many people were coming to this thing. Simpson was evasive over the phone, saying he would explain when he arrived. He stood outside the entrance of the building, his jacket slung over his shoulder looking towards the Pier Head where a huge white cruise liner was moored. More tourists were pouring out of the terminal building and heading towards town. Others were having their photographs taken at the latest statue to appear of four young men who came from the city and had made it a global brand long before the term had been invented.

'Excuse me, are you Mr McCarthy?'

'Yes'

'I'm Susy, Guy's assistant, he said to look out for you. We need to go in now and get started.' She had a set of earphones and attached microphone dangling around her neck and carried a clipboard. She shook his hand and they entered the building. Everywhere people were running around with clipboards and others were taping down cables along floors. They entered a large seated area and walked towards the stage which looked out across the Pier Head taking in the waterfront, cruise ship and tourists. Men were setting up cameras and lights and Guy Simpson was busy telling a group of staff that they had an hour before they were on air so they had better get things sorted out promptly. He noticed Mike and Susy and headed straight for them.

'Mike, great to see you, Susy, grab us a coffee and have a word with those makeup people about a tie for Mike, nothing too flash.' He shook Mike's hand, ushering him towards the seating.

'Listen mate, I'm eternally grateful for this big favour. As I walked in the office this morning I was told that the show was now going out on television, live for God's sake. It's not that I can't do it of course, it's just that we normally get a few days' notice. It's the result, Leave, biggest news story since Adam met Eve and the world's gone fuckin' crazy.'

Mike couldn't quite take all this in and wondered why he had suddenly become Guy Simpson's 'mate' and why this narcissistic control freak seemed to be behaving like he had an hour of his life left to live.

'Listen Guy, just what do you want me to do here?' Two workmen trotted past holding a huge studio light between them. Guy sighed and said, 'You will be on a panel with four politicians. I will be the adjudicator, a bit like your thing at the school except it will be much more controlled, obviously. We will have a live audience and

17

questions will come from them, well some of them. Don't worry, we will be having breaks during news reports on how the day is unfolding, we'll lead you through it Mike, no need to worry, it will be just like a radio show except on the TV.'

Mike shook his head, 'Guy, I'm just an ordinary fellah, I can't compete with politicians, they'll eat me alive.'

'No, you're not here for that. You're here to give the ordinary man's point of view. Let the politico's slag it out amongst themselves, I'll be winding them up to do so. Every now and then I'll go over to you and ask for your opinion. As you're a Remain man, on the losing side, you're in a great position to give your side of things without being too political. I saw you in action at the school, you're perfect for the part.'

'And who do you introduce me as? Mike McCarthy, local art teacher, as everyone wonders what the hell I'm doing here. I can imagine Joe Blogs sitting at home, watching daytime TV, and saying to his Missus, "who's this no-mark?"'

'No, we've got that sorted, this is the clever part. I'll introduce you as a local Remain Campaign manager, teacher, Europhile and cosmopolitan. You'll be interesting, yet elusive, just what we're looking for.'

Susy turned up with the coffees and a navy-blue tie for Mike.

'Come on, I'll tell you more about it in makeup.'

'Makeup… Me, oh come on Guy.'

Whatever else he thought of the media, Mike admired their professionalism. With just about 50 minutes to go before a major live broadcast everyone slotted in to their specialism whether it was presenting the show, camera operators, lighting bods, assistant producers, electricians, carpenters, makeup artists, or gofers like the ever-available Susy. As they walked Guy asked her to do just about everything which she either jotted down on a clipboard or spoke into her microphone for others to expedite. Finally, as they reached makeup he asked her where his suit was. Without looking up from her clipboard she informed him that it had just arrived from the cleaners and was hanging up in the changing room.

As they entered Mike saw a well-known former cabinet minister in a chair, head back. A large middle-aged woman with a mop of red hair was dabbing something on his cheeks. Facing him was a tall elegant lady, arms folded. One of the ever-present assistants with his clipboard stood to her side. She was sharing a joke with the politician along the lines that this makeup lady could take 20 years off him. She then headed towards Mike and Guy.

'Guy, this must be your Remain man?'

'Jennifer Hampson, producer. We are delighted to have you here. Has Guy filled you in about the show?'

No handshake, the arms folded again. She looked him straight in the eye.

'Yes, I think I've got it.'

'Good... I'm afraid your side lost Mr McCarthy, however, you will be in the best of company, the gentleman I was just speaking with is in the Remain camp.' She turned to her side, one arm out towards the politician. 'He will be getting the hard questions today; you can rest easy.'

'No, he bloody wont!' said the former cabinet minister. 'I've been up half the bloody night giving interviews.' They smiled at each other, the producer laughed telling him that if he didn't behave himself she'd tell the makeup lady to put the 20 years back on him.

He was waving his makeup lady away. 'Dinner tonight Jennifer? I know this city like the back of my hand.'

'Don't be silly Jack, I have to be back in Manchester by 5 pm. In case you hadn't noticed there's quite a big news story doing the rounds. You're not the only one who's been up half the night.'

She shook Mike's hand. 'Thank you again, relax and enjoy it Mr McCarthy, Guy's people will be close at hand for you.' She left, the assistant scurrying after her.

Guy and Mike took the two vacant chairs and were covered in plastic sheets; the large lady, now finished with her politician, came over.

'Hello Lovie' she said to him in a strong cockney accent. 'I'm Maggie, nothing much to this darlin', we just get you ready for the camera lights.' A few minutes of dabbing and she was done.

'Pop your leather jacket and tie on dear and let me have a look at you.'

Mike saw that Guy was being attended to by two attractive girls, one dabbing his face, the other doing something with his hands. The thought crossed his mind that the 'Sixth-Former' might be slightly envious at this scene and he allowed himself a rueful smile. He was beginning to enjoy himself. Maggie returned after rummaging through a massive aluminium trunk with a jar in her hand.

'I'll just rub some of this over your jacket... It stops the reflection of the lights. We don't get many gentlemen in leather jackets these days, I like them on gents, reminds me of the olden days. This is a lovely one dearie, had it a few years then?'

Mike amused her, 'Must be about 30 years, I got it in...' He paused for a moment. 'Germany.'

'Lovely... I can tell a good one when I sees one. Mr Burton always wore a nice soft leather in interviews; used to have them delivered to the studios by some place up in Jermyn Street. Handmade they was for 'im. Had to use this stuff on him before he went on.'

Mike didn't have a clue what she was talking about as she walked him over to a full-length mirror, 'There... You look a picture dearie, if you don't mind me sayin' so.' She put the top back on the jar and as she walked away she said,

'He had such a lovely voice though, I could listen to him all day.'

Guy Simpson emerged from the changing room immaculate in a petrol-blue suit, white shirt and lime green tie. Mike felt a little underdressed and said so.

'No, you're perfect Mike, I love the leather jacket, nice touch. Jenny Hampson is pleased too, I can tell... Believe me, it takes a lot to please her.'

He checked his watch.

'OK, twenty minutes to go, let's get on the floor and I'll introduce you to my team.'

They walked along the corridors together back towards the auditorium. Guy was collecting compliments from passing members of the production team as the faithful Susy caught up with them.

'You're good to go Guy, team now waiting for you... You look fantastic, you too, Mike.'

Mike thought he should thank her, especially as Simpson seemed to ignore her.

'Thanks Susy but it's really down to your makeup lady... Maggie I think her name is.'

Without looking around Simpson said, 'She's one of the best in the game, done Pinewood and all the TV shows in her time, even spent some time in Hollywood. Apparently, Richard Burton always asked for her, wouldn't have anyone else. We're lucky to have her, that's one of her granddaughters who was making me look beautiful.'

They entered the auditorium which had been transformed while they were away. The lighting was amazing, the cameras in place and manned in front of the stage area. The public were filing into their seats overseen by Jennifer Hampson, her trusty assistant and a team of stewards. Guy walked over to the audience just to the side of Hampson's crew. He waved to a couple of people he seemed to know then ushered Mike and Susy towards the stage area.

Mike asked, 'Where do you manage to get so many people at such short notice?'

Susy answered. 'We have a list of people we can call on and we have the universities. Students are always keen, especially when we give them a free sandwich and coffee.'

Three women came towards them, all with the ubiquitous headphones hung around their necks.

'Ah, my special girls,' said Guy.

'Mike, my ladies will look after you from now on... they will be at your beck and call all the time you are out there. Look after them and they will look after you. Same for you ladies, Mike's a special guest of mine so treat him well.' He winked at them.

He turned towards Mike, patted his arm and said. 'I want to thank you, Mike, I have a feeling this is going to be a big day for you and all of us, catch you later, good luck.'

He walked off to the stage area where the former cabinet minister was sitting and a group of assistants and gofers were milling about. One of Guy's ladies introduced herself as Alex, an assistant producer. She and the others walked him towards his seat on the stage. Whilst one of her colleagues slipped a small pack on a wire down the back of his jacket another placed her earphones on her head. The pack was clipped onto the side of his belt and she carefully placed a small earphone in his ear. All the time Alex was explaining what was happening.

'We'll keep speaking Mike whilst the girls adjust the sound. I'll be up at the back with Jenny listening and watching everything. I'll give you instructions, but only when necessary such as when we are counting down to the start and breaks. Don't answer me, just carry on as normal, don't feel rushed or concerned about anything. The girls will be close by, off camera listening. If I need them to do anything they will help. For instance, if your earpiece isn't working just tap on your ear and one of them will come to you. Don't worry, the camera won't be on you, we'll go to one of the other guests. I know this is your first time but you'll find as soon as we get under way you'll be fine.'

She was reassuringly calm and confident. 'Any questions?'

'About two million.' He could hear her assistants laughing in his earphone and Alex gave him a wide smile.

'You know Mike, one of the things in life I love is when we work in this city. The sense of humour is incredible. It can overcome just about anything. Just keep nice and natural as you are now and you'll be brilliant. See you later.'

They departed and he looked over where Guy was being wired up. Susy was doing her sound checks with him. The politicians were going through the same routine and the former cabinet minister looked over and nodded to him. He heard Jennifer Hampson's voice come into his ear.

'Two minutes everyone, two minutes.'

The assistants started to move away and the cameras came in closer. One of Alex's girls gave him a smile and a thumbs-up gesture as she walked to the side of the stage. The countdown began with Alex's voice and Guy Simpson looked directly into the central camera.

'Five, four, three, two, one...'

'Good afternoon Britain, Europe and across the globe on this famous day. You join us from Liverpool, a city that has throughout its history reached out to the world just as we reach out to you, today...'

He closed the front door behind him and dropped his briefcase and jacket in the hallway. Exhausted, he headed for the living room at the back of the house and flopped into an easy chair. He had maybe an hour before the kids and Jane came in. Perhaps he could sleep for an hour in the chair. Impossible; he never could sleep without lying down however tired he was.

He felt that his first and maybe his last television appearance had gone surprisingly well. Alex was right, as soon as things had started he relaxed and went along with things. The Remain camp were well represented with the ex-cabinet minister, a local MP and himself. The Leavers included a senior member of UKIP and a pugnacious political journalist from one of the daily tabloid newspapers. Mike hadn't been in full agreement with the two Remain politicians on certain matters and fought his corner, telling them they had underestimated and even patronised working-class voters in South Wales, The North East, Lancashire and Yorkshire. Many of these people had voted Leave as a protest vote against a lack of investment in the post-industrial world. He argued that this was a vote by the ordinary man in the street and refuted the suggestion from the Leavers that it was all about immigration, just look at the cities and areas that had voted to Remain – wealthy, cosmopolitan university cities and London, all teeming with immigrants. Compare these places to the Leave areas, run-down, insular, white, working class with aging communities and in many cases, few immigrants. This had brought loud applause and cheers from the audience along with a smirk and smile from Guy Simpson who then had his 'politicos' fighting it out amongst themselves over Mike's points.

But as he stretched out in the chair he wondered just what was going to happen to his country. No one knew for certain at this stage how things would pan out. We were only a few hours into Brexit, this was going to be a long hard road. We had lost a prime minister but the government would have some sort of exit strategy in place and while he had been mixing in the rarefied atmosphere of the media everyone from the governor of the Bank of England down would be doing some sort of damage limitation exercise.

He heard the front door close and Sam walked into the room.

'Hi Dad... Were you on the tele?'

Mike smiled. 'Yeah, just a small part... Who told you?'

'All my mates are talking about it on Facebook, and Georgie just texted me.'

He showed Mike a picture of the panel from the show. There he was, on the end looking out towards the audience. Sam left as Mike's own phone buzzed. It was a message from Rachel Evans.

Well done Michael! Just heard that you were marvellous. Pop in on Monday and tell me all about it. R.E.

He could hazard a guess who had told her.

The front door again and Georgie came in. 'Dad, what the hell! Got a new career? You were fab by all accounts, how come you did that?' She was looking at her phone whilst speaking. 'I'm getting loads of messages about it, OMG! Here you are speaking on Twitter! Does Mum know?'

Mike shook his head but smiled, he was too old for all this he thought. He could hear his own voice coming from Georgie's phone as she laughed and whooped.

'I'm so proud of you Dad.' She turned and said, 'Got to get in the shower, off-out tonight.' Georgie, like most teenagers could change the world and come back to earth again, all in the space of a couple of seconds.

Sam returned stuffing a small rucksack with toiletries, earphones and Xbox games.

'I'm going to Jamie's for a sleepover tonight, Mum knows.'

'Yeah, she told me, do you need a lift?'

'Yes, ok, but it's too early, I'm not leaving for about half an hour... Dad... What's going to happen now we are leaving Europe?'

'Well we're not sailing off into the middle of the Atlantic and for the time being nothing much will change.' He tried to make light of things, Sam was a sensitive, serious boy and had followed the Referendum campaign a bit too intensively for a 14-year-old.

'No, I don't mean how we will go about leaving, I mean what about things here at home? There were a few problems with the Polish kids in school today.'

'What sort of problems?'

'Oh, some of the Leave kids were ribbing them about going home, probably just banter, it's just that most of them were born here.'

Mike felt himself getting annoyed, he raised his voice, 'Nothing's going to happen to those kids Sam, they were born here and have every right to be in our country. Don't worry, as soon as things die down people will forget all about Brexit.' He didn't believe his own words and Sam looked at him sceptically.

He heard Jane come in, Sam went into the hall to meet her, Mike followed.

She kissed Sam on the forehead and Mike on the cheek. Mike and Jane walked into the kitchen together. Jane went to the fridge and took out a carton of orange juice.

Mike asked her how her day had been while wondering how she managed to look so smart after a day in a primary school. He felt ragged.

She took a drink of orange juice and handed him a glass. 'Fine, no problems… Oh, Sinead and Tim…'

Mike sighed and frowned, 'I forgot about them…'

Jane interrupted, 'No, they've cancelled, their eldest boy is down with tonsillitis, I should have texted you, sorry. Don't worry, we'll sort something out later, Sam's going on a sleepover and Georgie's out tonight. I'll give Sam a lift.'

Mike cheered up. He was starting to feel very tired and could do without the socialising tonight.

Sam stood at the door, rucksack at the ready indicating he was ready to leave for Jamie's.

He sat in the kitchen where the day had started, rubbed his eyes and undid his tie. He couldn't believe what had happened overnight although he had predicted that the Leave side would win. When friends and colleagues had suggested that he was wrong and that Remain would win, perhaps comfortably, he had simply smiled, shrugged his shoulders and said, 'wait and see.' He drew no consolation from the fact he had been right yet sometimes he had thought, no, hoped he would get it wrong. He had based his prediction on many factors but the main one was the campaign itself. The Leave side appealed to people's base emotions, xenophobia, immigration, crime and terrorism, sometimes bordering dangerously close to racial hatred. In addition, they got the message across that the average person would somehow be better off financially. Nonsense of course but the real guilty party was the Remain camp. They fought a hopelessly inept and fragmented campaign and seemed to believe that people would simply vote the way they requested. This was a dangerous game that had backfired spectacularly, the damage caused could take years to repair.

Georgie came in wearing a long white dressing gown, her hair wrapped in a towel. She whistled a tune as she sat at the kitchen table painting her nails. Mike watched her wishing he could be as detached and unaffected by the world as she was. Or was she? Perhaps it was simply her age. She broke his reverie.

'How did you manage to get on the TV programme Dad? What was it like?'

'It's a long story, Guy Simpson who was at the school debate contacted school and asked for me. As for what it was like, it's hard to say, I was incredibly nervous before it started but once it got going I felt fine and enjoyed myself, in a funny sort of way.'

Jane came back and joined them both.

'Hi Mum, did you know we have a TV star in the family?'

'Sam's just mentioned it in the car, but you know Sam, a man of few words, all he said was Dad was on the television and left it at that, is it right Mike?'

'I'm afraid so and before you ask it was Rachel's idea, I haven't gone freelance just yet.'

Georgie jumped up and said, 'He'll tell you all about it while I go and get ready, *ciao*.'

Jane took off her suit jacket, took his hand and led him into the lounge saying, 'right, tell me all and don't spare the details.' So he did.

After half an hour Jane got up and made them both some tea which she brought into the lounge on a tray. She was smiling and shaking her head.

Laughing, she said, 'So what happens next, *The politics Show, Newsnight, Channel 4 News?*'

He kept his face straight as he said, 'To start with yes, then onto the European capitals as the BBCs Chief Political editor, after that I'm off to the States for the presidential election.'

She slid closer to him on the settee, took hold of his tie and brushed her lips against his ear. She whispered, 'They'll have to get past me first and where did you get that tie? I always buy your ties.'

He kissed her gently on the lips and said quietly, 'A very pretty young lady gave it to me and said I could keep it as a souvenir.' He kissed her again.

'Oh, come on you two, how old are you? Well, what do you think?'

They broke apart like a couple of guilty teenagers as Georgie stood there before them in a short black cocktail dress, high heels and a clutch bag. Her dark hair was piled high and a silver necklace completed her outfit.

Jane recovered first. 'Georgie, you look beautiful, what else can I say?'

Both women looked at Mike who seemed bewildered.

'Where are you going Georgie?' He looked from one to the other as if their silence would answer his question.

'I'm going out for a special meal for my 18th birthday, Dad, now do you like my outfit?'

'Yeah, it's lovely, but hang on, you're not 18 for two weeks.'

'I know but he's going home to Surrey on Sunday and won't be here for my birthday.'

A car horn sounded from somewhere, Mike still bewildered said, 'He... Who, who's going to Surrey?'

'That sounds like my taxi, I'm off.' She bent over and kissed her parents before leaving.

Mike said, 'Who's she talking about Jane, who's taking her out?'

'Matt of course... Apparently, you've met him, they've been seeing each other for a few weeks now.'

'Matt, I don't know anyone called Matt... Oh, hang on, the student, the lad at the debate, but he must be 22 or 23.'

Jane sighed, 'And she's 18 Michael, I would say that ratio's just about perfect, wouldn't you?'

She picked up the tray, took it out to the kitchen and returned. Mike was standing looking out of the French windows. Jane came up behind him whispering, 'As the kids are out tonight and we're no longer meeting Sinead and Tim how about I order some Chinese food and we have a quiet night in?' She put her arms around his waist, he turned and faced her, cupped her face in his hands and kissed her gently. 'I need a shower first.' She purred, hooked one of her legs around his and said, 'We both do... Together.'

Later in the evening they had watched some news reports together until Jane had gone off to bed telling him not to stay up too late. On *Newsnight* there was a discussion about the impact of the Referendum on Europe and their reporter interviewed French political figures. Some of them were quite bitter about the result, fearing the encouragement it would give to certain extremists in France. Others were grudgingly resigned to it yet alluded to it being typically British to stab their friends in the back. Mike thought that they were being polite, the French establishment would be furious at the result and its possible knock-on effects on their economy and domestic politics.

He was thinking what a strange, yet significant day it had been. There had been others in his life and like today, they had made him what he was and what he believed in. The pictures from Paris continued and his eyelids began to close. France, it had been too long.

Chapter 3
1979

The seagulls swooped towards him. Their squawking always reminded him of home, wherever he was. As a child, he feared them, yet as he grew older he took a more belligerent stance. He took that stance now, waving his arm at one that came in at head height. The bus driver looked up from stowing luggage, laughed, mimicked Mike's arm action and spoke in French, to himself and anyone else who might want to listen. He called a woman forward with her suitcase which he took from her, laughed, pretending to be unable to lift her luggage because of its heavy weight. Then he scooped it up with one hand before laying it gently in the hold, took a bow and received mock applause from the waiting passengers. He gestured Mike forward with his bag, an old canvas Belgian army rucksack bought for £2.50 in his local Army surplus store. Seeing the rucksack, the driver pointed at it, then to himself and mimed carrying it on his back whilst pretending to mop his brow. The other passengers roared with laughter, yet Mike couldn't see the joke, his schoolboy French unable to keep up with a language that to him, was spoken much too fast. A fellow passenger, a middle-aged woman, intervened waving her hand in front of the driver and giving him a mouthful in French. She took Mike's arm, walking him back to the others saying in heavily accented English, 'Jean-Michel is a fool, always was and always will be young one.' A clown, maybe but like most clowns Mike suspected there was something much deeper behind the façade. The luggage stored, the driver shouted 'Paris', 'Paris', as everyone boarded the Calais to Paris coach.

Apart from a couple of trips to Ireland, which he didn't count, his first time in a foreign country saw him sitting on a wonderful old bus that looked as though it was left over from the 1940s. Gleaming chrome and polished paintwork outside with burgundy leather seats inside made him feel like he had gone back in time. The old coach drove past some semi-derelict cottages on the edge of the dock area before heading onto a wide boulevard with some stately old houses on each side of the road. He was keen to take everything in and scanned around at the cars, the pedestrians, the road signs, shops and cafes. Already, and only 20 miles away from England he felt not only in a different country, but in a different world.

The bus soon left the town behind and travelled along straight narrow roads lined with poplar trees. All around the land was flat with hardly a hedge or a tree except for an occasional clump. The weather was warmer here with irrigation sprays satisfying thirsty crops in the adjacent fields. He pulled a book out of his shoulder bag and laid it on the empty seat next to him. Suddenly, he felt tired, glanced at his watch and realised he had been travelling for over 12 hours. He had left Liverpool at 4 am, taken an early train to London, walked from Euston Station to a bus station on Pentonville Road and after a short break for a sandwich and a cup of tea taken a bus to Ramsgate to catch the hovercraft to Calais. He ate a bar of chocolate he had kept in his bag for the journey and finished some lukewarm tea from a thermos flask he had made before leaving home that morning. The bus journey would take four hours to reach Paris. He closed his eyes and put his head back.

He was proudly working class, the only child of a Liverpool Docker, yet one thing he was grateful for from his father was a strong emphasis on the value of education. If ever his father had any spare money he would buy a book, usually reference books or biographies of historical and political figures. Mike had a small home library at his disposal and this had helped him through school and into teacher training college. He was currently training to become an art teacher at a college in the south of the city, travelling daily from his parent's home in the Anfield area. When he had told his parents that he intended to travel to Paris his mother was concerned yet his father had been extremely encouraging and supportive. Together, they had sat down planning the journey and discussing places to visit. Not that his father, James McCarthy, had ever visited Paris or for that matter, anywhere else in mainland Europe, but he always said that travel broadened the mind and was keen for his son to see Europe. He added that if the ordinary working people of Europe had been able to visit each other's countries before 1914 and 1939 then much of the xenophobic antagonism that led to two world wars may have been avoided.

His father had been largely self-taught and in his younger days had mixed with some of the city's working class, self-taught, Marxist activists who fought for better housing, wages and workers' rights. A major influence on the young James was a family friend, George Garrett. Garrett was one of those interesting, mid-war, working-class writers from Liverpool who had started out as a seaman and Docker before going on to become a writer of essays, novels and plays. It was Garrett who had advised James on the importance of travel and the observation of different cultures around the world. Unable to put this into practice himself, he had every intention of persuading his son to do so.

'Monsieur, Monsieur, please wake, we have stopped.'

Mike rubbed his eyes and looked up to see his female saviour from Calais who was tapping him on the shoulder from the aisle. He looked about and saw only countryside.

'Not Paris?' he said sleepily.

'No, not yet, a stop to eat only.'

He walked from the bus to a rustic inn that appeared to be the only building in sight. The land was still flat except at the back of the inn was a tree covered ridge that ran parallel to the road. The inn turned out to be a restaurant with plain wooden tables that a woman and girl were quickly laying with gingham table cloths. Mike picked a table and sat down. The young waitress, a girl of about 18, came across to lay the table and he watched her as she smoothed out the tablecloth, laid out cutlery and left the menu. She had olive-coloured skin and wavy, raven black hair. He thanked her in French to which she replied, '*De rein Monsieur, Je suis Jeanette.*'

'May we join you?' a voice said in English.

31

Two aging English ladies sat down opposite him and introduced themselves. They had suspected he was English when they saw him at Calais and offered their services as translators of the menu. The waitress returned with a jug of water and a basket of bread, laying out two further places for the ladies. They told him they had been coming to the restaurant for many years and the Calais to Paris bus always stopped off here for an hour during the journey. He ordered chicken soup on the recommendation of the older of the two ladies who said that the dish was a house speciality. He looked around the restaurant to see the bus driver kissing both waitresses on the cheeks in the French way before the chef appeared and both men embraced in a hug. The elder of the ladies explained that their driver Jean-Michel and Paul the chef had served in the army together in Vietnam and Algeria and had remained friends since. The two waitresses were his wife and daughter.

The soup was magnificent. In a large bowl with whole pieces of chicken, it resembled a casserole and tasted better than any soup he had tasted before. Mike asked both ladies about their journey and they told him they travelled to Paris every summer by the same route, stayed in the same hotel near the Gare du Nord and visited the galleries and theatres of Paris. After his meal, he excused himself, paid and thanked the young waitress before going outside to stretch his legs. He had about twenty minutes before he needed to be back on the bus and wandered off towards the ridge at the back of the building. A small paved pathway led to the top through the trees and he thread his way upwards to an open area on the top of the ridge. It was a sight that would forever live with him.

After ten minutes, he returned to the small carpark and lit a cigarette. Looking across the road, through the poplar trees he saw more of them. Little white walls with white dots and a flag planted in the centre. He counted four this time stretching off into the distance. On the ridge, he had looked out to a sea of white dots, graves of thousands of soldiers from the Great War, the flags in the centre of the cemeteries told of boys from Canada, Britain and France who had fallen fighting in the 'War to End All Wars'. Unfortunately, that conflict didn't end war and for the last half century Europe and much of the world had been in a state of almost permanent warfare. Some people obviously hadn't heeded the warning of these graves. He pulled on his cigarette, dropped it on the ground and put his foot on it. Looking around he saw the passengers leaving the restaurant and starting to drift back towards the bus. When Jean-Michel had counted them all back they set off towards Paris.

The sun was dipping low over the flat fields as the old bus headed south. Mike saw many more cemeteries; some tiny with maybe 30 or 40 graves, others in the distance covering vast tracts of land; the late sunshine turned the west facing gravestones deathly pink, orange then blood red. Most of the flags were the French tricolour, others, British, Canadian and Australian. Occasionally, there was the odd flag that he struggled to recognise but Mike was certain he spotted the Indian and Algerian flags, testimony to a world conflict. As the sun began to set they entered Paris.

Mike moved to the window seat to get a better view as the bus drove up onto the Périphérique and he just managed to make out the Eiffel Tower in the fading light. Half a mile later they came off the elevated roadway and entered the Barbès area in the north of the city. He was amazed at how many people were about. The cafes were packed both inside and outside. Aproned waiters wove their way through the tables with trays full of drinks for socialising groups. Couples stood on street corners embracing and acknowledging car horns with a wave. The city was alive and vibrant and he was enraptured.

The driver shouted something which Mike supposed was their first stop as some passengers were starting to stand up and take bags from the overhead shelf. The two English women wished him a pleasant stay in Paris and Mike asked them should he be getting off here. They checked his ticket and told him that he was booked on till the Gare de l'Est which was the next stop along. The coach pulled into the side of the Gare du Nord and most of the passengers alighted. Mike could hear Jean-Michel getting their luggage out of the hold and saying goodbye. They got going again and straight away he heard the driver shout 'Gare de l'Est.' After a short journey around the block the coach pulled into a small carpark next to the station. Mike saw Jean-Michel get his jacket from behind his seat and heard him opening the luggage compartment. Mike stepped down off the coach and went to the luggage area as the driver was waving goodbye to the other passengers. Jean-Michel placed his rucksack in front of him and said in perfect English. 'Have you arranged somewhere to stay in Paris?'

Somewhat taken aback Mike said, 'You speak English?'

'I suspect a little better than your French, my friend.'

Mike said, 'I have an address of a small hotel that may be suitable, but I haven't booked it.' He showed the driver the address and telephone number on a small piece of paper. The driver shook his head saying, 'This is a very busy time in Paris, you should have booked. Come with me, we will call them to see if they have any rooms.' Mike put his rucksack on his back and together they walked into the station. They walked to a café and Jean-Michel put his briefcase on an outside table before going to the counter and speaking to a waiter. It was obvious they knew each other as there was an instant rapport between them. Jean-Michel came back and told Mike to wait while he went and phoned the hotel. The waiter came over with two bottles of beer which he placed on the table yet Mike was still wondering how Jean-Michel spoke such fine English. He sipped at the beer which was very cold and tasted wonderful. He looked at his watch, 9:30 pm and the station was very busy with passengers even at this late hour, and he heard singing on one of the platforms. Looking over, he saw hundreds of soldiers singing. They were dressed in immaculate uniforms as if about to go on parade and some were drinking bottles of beer.

Jean-Michel returned, sat down at the table and took a large gulp of beer.

'This hotel is fully booked but don't worry I have a solution.'

The coach driver had told him he had telephoned his cousin who was the manager of a small hotel on the Boulevard Saint-Germain and she had a room available for Mike. It would be cheaper than the original hotel he had in mind and included breakfast. He would be able to take the Metro to Saint-Germain-des- Prés and it was a short walk from there. Jean-Michel wrote down the details on a piece of paper and gave him a small plastic Metro plan. Mike was more than grateful for his help yet was still intrigued about his excellent English.

'That's fantastic, I can't thank you enough, but I must ask you, how come you speak such good English?'

The older man looked him in the eyes, called over the waiter and ordered more drinks.

'Well Veronique said to give her a couple of hours to get the room ready, so you asked, I will tell you.'

He was from an agricultural family near the city of Tours on the river Loire. They were tenant farmers, not poor, but not rich either. They farmed 100 acres of land for the local landowner, kept enough for themselves and their animals to eat and could sell a small number of crops at market. Their ancient farmhouse was their own, bequeathed to the family by the current landowner's ancestor after he had returned from military service with Bonaparte. Jean-Michel was an only child, 14, when World War Two started and his father had been excused military service because he was a wounded veteran of the first war and was needed in the fields. He helped his father on the land when he wasn't in school along with a few other local boys.

The situation with the occupying power was one of live and let live. They hardly saw a German soldier and any notifications for the local populace were pinned to the police station door in the local village. In mid-1942 two things happened that would change the bus driver's life forever. One Sunday morning several of the boys who worked on the land failed to appear at the farm. Two younger boys did turn up and told the farmer and his son that two of the boys had been taken away by the Germans for forced labour, whilst two others had run away from home when they heard about the round-ups. That evening Jean-Michel packed a haversack with essential items and spare clothing and hid it in a small copse that led to the hills at the back of the farm house. He didn't tell his parents what he had done.

During that week, Jean-Michel and his father went to the local market to sell their produce. Afterwards, his father went to a local café to meet some friends and Jean wandered into a small square where local teenagers gathered. He got talking to a girl his own age and her 18-year-old brother who told him that more young men had been taken against their will and they both intended to head south and join the resistance. Jean felt that this was a drastic step but asked them how they would find the resistance. The girl replied, 'They will find you.' She then whispered something to Jean before leaving.

On the journey back to the farm, their pony and cart was stopped by a French policeman on a bicycle. Jean's father asked what was happening and was told that the Germans were carrying out a raid at a nearby farm, looking for 'bandits'. As he spoke shots rang out across the fields from the direction of the farm. His father calmed the horse as Jean looked towards the farm building where a young man in black trousers and a white shirt ran into the adjacent fields. He was followed by two French gendarmes, one of whom fired his pistol into the air. The man kept running towards the nearest hedge cover when several German soldiers came out of the building, took aim with their rifles and shot the fugitive five metres short of the hedge line.

That night Jean-Michel lay in his bed fully clothed. At 11 pm he crept downstairs in his bare feet. He quietly picked up his boots and socks and put some bread, sausage and cheese in his jacket pockets before slipping out of the backdoor of the farmhouse. He walked the half mile to the wooded hillock where he found the haversack he had hidden a few nights earlier. He checked it carefully and found its contents undisturbed. He now had a bottle of water, a torch, penknife, some fishing line, hooks, snares and spare clothing as well as an old map of central France. He settled down against a tree and waited in complete darkness.

A few minutes after midnight he saw two sets of headlights heading down the lane towards his farm. He stood up, turned around and with eyes now completely adjusted to the darkness he headed off in a southerly direction. The girl had been right when she had whispered to him in the village square. She told him they would come for him tonight.

Mike bought him another beer and a coffee for himself. Entirely taken with the bus driver's story he asked him to continue.

'I walked due south, always at night and slept up during the day. I ate berries and fruit and drank water from clean streams until I entered what used to be called Vichy France but was just a hotbed of collaborationists. I got work on a farm with some other boys who were on the run from the north. The farmer didn't care, he got his cheap labour in return for food and lodgings in a barn. After a couple of weeks, I met a couple of men in a café in the local village. They were Resistance, and that night they picked me up in a truck and we headed into the hills west of Limoges.

'For the next few months I lived in safe houses, in woods and hills. We raided police stations to get weapons and generally made a nuisance of ourselves for Vichy and the Germans. We lacked control and leadership until later in the year the Allies started landing agents, arms and supplies. I was given the job of looking after an English radio-operator who had been parachuted in with others to coordinate the Resistance. His name was James Rayner, 21 years, and his French was about as good as yours Michael,' he said with a smile.

'We had to keep constantly on the move from safe houses to small camps in the hills. We had little else to do but hide and transmit messages so he taught me to speak English. These were good times for us attacking train lines with plastique, killing Germans and Vichy scum. Then the Germans began to move Gestapo and SS troops into the area and things got difficult. They would sweep the hills and forests catching many of our boys. Many were betrayed by collaborationists, traitors and good French men and women who were tortured for information. They would then hang our comrades in the local towns and villages as a deterrent. If the agents and radio operators were caught they would be tortured for infor-mation, sent to a concentration camp and executed.'

Mike listened with fascination and horror as Jean spoke, but let him continue.

'James and myself kept on the move constantly, trusting nobody. We had to abandon two radio sets as the enemy got close to us. He smashed the insides with a hammer of one set, another we threw into a river. It became difficult to link up with other agents and groups as the Germans flooded the Resistance areas with troops, police and Gestapo thugs. James's French got better and we were like brothers to the point that we pretended to be brothers. It wasn't all one sided; we had our Sten guns, plastic-explosive, commando knives and stashes of ammunition that we kept buried in various locations. We laughed, loved and yes, killed together. Neither of us had any doubts about what we were involved in. We knew we could be captured, tortured and hung at any time so we made sure to kill first. It was war, Michael.'

Mike looked at Jean who was taking another gulp of beer.

'Do you still keep in touch with James?'

Jean looked at Mike, took a packet of French cigarettes from his pocket and offered him one. The bus driver lit one each and took a draw. Mike would never forget the aroma of the smoke. Jean-Michel continued speaking.

'As D-Day drew near we were kept busy. Our group attacked railway lines, blew up trees that blocked roads, attacked German convoys and police units wherever we found them. This was another good time for us. We had plenty of weapons that were flown in by your RAF or stolen from dead Germans. Our Sten guns had been adapted to use captured ammunition and there was a feeling that victory was just around the corner. The Germans had moved their best troops to the north to fight the Allies when they landed and new agents were parachuted in to pull us all together. When the Allies invaded, we believed the end of the war was only a few days away. The Germans began to move heavy armoured forces up from the south towards Normandy. These were front line SS troops and it was our job to slow them and stop them anyway we could to help our brothers fighting on the beaches. At that time, we were in the hills close to a small town called Tulle in central France. The area was controlled by Communist resistance groups who we didn't trust but would help each other out occasionally. They had plenty of men but few weapons so we arranged weapon drops in return for them helping to attack the Germans.'

TESCO

HESWALL 0345 0700081

GIFTCARD	£10.00
TOTAL	£10.00
Visa SALE	£10.00

Visa contactless))))

AID	: A0000000031010	
NUMBER	: ***********9686	ICC
PAN SEQ NO	: 01	
AUTH CODE	: 004915	
MERCHANT	: 46267272	
CHANGE DUE		£0.00

CLUBCARD STATEMENT

CLUBCARD NUMBER ***************4782	
QUALIFYING SPEND	£0.00
POINTS THIS VISIT	0
TOTAL UP TO 20/07/17	674

A chance to win a £1000 Tesco Gift Card
by telling us about your trip
at www.tescoviews.com
and collect 25 Clubcard points.
Terms and conditions apply,
please see website for details.

22/07/17 17:06 2672 091 4005 6397

Mike and Jean shared another cigarette as Jean looked at his watch and continued.

'The Communist fighters attacked Tulle and to start with did well, taking the garrison prisoner and liberating the town. We were up in the hills transmitting messages to London, asking for more air drops when we heard heavy weapons and artillery. Waffen SS troops had attacked Tulle to retake it from us and many of our fighters were starting to retreat to the hills. As they reached us the Germans began to fire artillery shells into our positions making things very uncomfortable. James sent messages asking for ammunition, medical supplies and reinforcements to be parachuted in as we fired our rifles and Stens at the Germans who had started to advance uphill. James sent his last message before smashing the radio with rocks. As he did so a shell exploded nearby.'

Both men looked at each other, Mike open-mouthed said, 'James?'

'We were ok, just deafened and shaken. The trees had absorbed most of the blast. We grabbed our weapons and headed off the other side of the hill before we were overwhelmed. We managed to find a barn as night fell, a few miles from the battle. We had not faced this type of warfare before, didn't have the men or the weapons to fight this type of conflict. Our success had depended on stealth and surprise, this was different. Two days later we linked up with other Resistance fighters in woods about 20 miles north of Tulle which was in a supply drop area. Many were wounded and in bad shape and some were our old Communist friends from Tulle. They told us after they had escaped the SS troops had rounded up the town's population and systematically hung dozens of men from lamp-posts while their loved ones were forced to look on. There were rumours that the SS had gone into villages near Limoges, killed everyone and burnt all the buildings to the ground. As we spoke the Royal Air Force began a big supply drop above us and we could replenish our supplies of weapons, ammunition, medical equipment and food. As soon as James and I had filled our haversacks we moved off before the enemy arrived. We had one objective. Paris.

'We had become detached from our group, lost our radio, were in unfamiliar territory, could trust nobody and were now fighting an enemy that had begun to slaughter the local population at will. We had a pistol and a Sten gun each with limited ammunition and just a few days of field rations. Although we had some silk maps of France, we had no idea where the Allies had advanced to or if the Germans had thrown them back into the sea. We were still well south of the Loire, travelled by night and slept in woods by day. We had decided to try to get to Paris, get in touch with Resistance groups and continue the fight in any way we could. We reverted to our stealth and evasion tactics that had served us so well in the past. Our main problem was food. We could fill up our water bottles from wells but had to snare rabbits to eat which held us up and could have exposed us when we lit fires to cook them. We couldn't steal food because again, this would have alerted the enemy although we did collect berries and apples which kept us going. We stole from bins at night and found a newspaper which told us that the Allies were bogged down in Normandy. So now we knew that eventually the Allies would win. We hadn't seen a German soldier since Tulle so it was obvious they had sent most of their men north to fight. This gave us heart but we knew we would soon have to cross the Loire and the closer we got to the river the more military activity we observed including Allied bombers pounding the enemy positions close to the bridges. We hid up in woods overlooking the river and tried to work out how to cross. We couldn't cross the remaining bridges as they were patrolled by Germans and we were too weak to swim such a wide river. A boat was the answer, but how? When night fell, we went as close to the shoreline as possible to see what was happening. Just downstream we saw some lights on the water and James focussed his binoculars on them. Fishermen in boats. We watched them for several hours until they sailed off. Two boats came close to our position then moored about 300 metres away on our bank. We waited until the occupants had left, waited another half hour then helped ourselves to a boat. By daylight we had walked several miles towards Paris.'

Mike was fascinated. He had never heard anything like this before. He looked at his watch but Jean-Michel reassured him that he had nearly finished his story. Mike, slightly embarrassed, urged him to continue. They both lit more cigarettes and the Frenchman continued.

'We had crossed near the town of Blois which is about half way between Tours and Orléans and headed for Paris. There was less tree cover now and the land was generally flatter. There were also more Germans about and Allied planes were constantly bombing them. We could only walk on roads at night and usually slept in dry ditches during the day for a few hours. We would either starve to death or reach Paris, we had no choice but to keep going. Eventually we reached the Foret de Fontainebleau and slept under trees. We were exhausted, dirty, hungry and dehydrated but had made it to the outskirts of Paris and were not going to give up now. The forest seemed empty and after we had rested we had a scout around, guns at the ready. We came across a large open area that looked as if it had recently been vacated by troops and their vehicles in a hurry. Camp fires had been hastily stamped out, there were tyre and tank tracks and rubbish piles strewn about. A check of the rubbish showed German ration packages. We carefully checked the wooded areas for trip wires and booby traps, the German's liked to leave nasty surprises for us when they moved camp. We had done the same to them back in south-west France with our plastic explosives. We used hand signals to communicate as we went from tree to tree. They had certainly been in a hurry to go and had left empty wooden crates and boxes strewn all over the place. Normally, when they moved camp they were so thorough we would never have known they had been there. We came across some wooden huts and again checked around for booby-traps. The huts had been built for the French army before the war and still had signs in French on the doors. We had to take care and it took us most of the day to search the camp. We were looking for anything that we could use, ammunition, weapons and food, but most of all food.'

'We found a kit bag with boxes of German field rations and gorged ourselves, found some old French army shirts, berets and pants that had been stored away since 1940 to change into. James found a Bakelite razor and some blades and we shaved off our beards at an outside tap. All the time we covered each other with our Stens and as soon as we were ready broke down the machine guns and put them in the bottom of the kit bag with the food and headed off for Paris. We had a plan of sorts, to follow the Seine into the city and try to link up with other Resistance fighters. We quickly made it down to the river and started to follow it north. I suppose we looked like a couple of workmen but felt completely exposed as we wandered along passing workmen and old ladies walking dogs. It had been weeks since we had any human contact and we were jumpy. Once or twice I reached for my pistol inside my jacket. We came to some small docks where a barge was unloading flour and James came up with a plan. I told the old captain that we would work our ticket on the barge into Paris. He laughed but agreed, saying he couldn't pay us but he would feed us and added we looked like we needed feeding. We helped with some unloading before setting off towards the city. We had our first meal for weeks that night on board that barge. The next morning, we docked just outside the city centre and the crew began to unload their cargo. The captain came to us with two old reefer jackets and told us to wear them because he doubted the pockets in our battered coats could hold our guns much longer. James was about to shoot him but the old man shook his head, raised his hands a little and pointed to his Great War medals on his tunic. He then gave James a piece of paper with the name of a café and told us to ask for 'Paul'.

'You were brave men,' said Mike.

'Not men, just boys, Michael. But well on the way to becoming men.' Jean looked at his watch and said, 'My wife will be meeting me here soon so I will finish off and then get you off to your hotel.' He continued.

'We walked into the city and it was then I realised how dreadful we must have looked. We had lost more than ten kilos each in weight. I had an old piece of rope tied around my waist to stop my reefer coat flapping open. James, always taller and heavier than me didn't look too bad with his beret and kitbag. We must have looked like half-starved sailors up from the docks, people were certainly giving us a wide berth.'

Jean laughed a little to himself, obviously recalling those special days. He finished his beer and continued.

'We found the café and 15 minutes later were taken upstairs into a room by several men who were obviously armed. They took our weapons from us and stood us in front of the man known as "Paul" who told us that if we failed to answer any of his questions the men would shoot us. This reassured us, it was classic Resistance activity that we both recognised. After we had told him our story he told us that we would be taken to a safe house, that he was now our commanding officer and we should wait for orders with our guns cleaned and ready for action. He finished off by telling us to rest and get something to eat. We shook hands and one of his men was told to take us to the "shop".

'The "shop" was a small haberdashery store near Saint-Sulpice, not far from where you will be staying in Paris, Michael. An old lady manned the counter and we were taken into the back where two girls about our own age were working at sewing machines. We were introduced by our guide, they were called Aimee and Claire and they took us upstairs to an attic with two beds. Aimee told us that we both smelled, that she would heat water and run a bath for us and pointed at James, smiled and said, "You first". When the bath was run James and Aimee went into the bathroom, she threw out his dirty clothes and locked the door behind her. Claire picked them up, looked at me and said, "You're next, with me."'

Jean-Michel was chuckling to himself, lighting cigarettes for both before saying, 'Paris girls, Michael, they are something special.'

'That night the girls made us the best dinner we had had for months, where they got the food from, I don't know, they even managed to find a bottle of wine from somewhere. They had looked through their supplies in the shop and found us some clothes to wear. It turned out they were cousins and the old lady at the front of the shop was an aunt whom they worked for repairing clothes. All three women were members of "Paul's" Resistance group and had helped hide fellow members on the run as well as Allied airmen and Jews for a short time before they were moved on.

'They told us that the Americans were getting close to the city and when the orders came the Resistance would rise up and overthrow the German garrison and their French collaborators.

Both girls were busy making tricolour armbands to be distributed to the fighters when the time came. James and myself were shocked by this and told them what had happened at Tulle together with other towns in Central France and what the Nazis had done to ordinary people. They didn't seem too bothered by this, explaining that most of the German troops had left Paris to fight the Allies and those remaining were second-rate soldiers and confined to barracks. Aimee said that the Gestapo and their spies would be dealt with in a "special way".

'James and I were itching to get back at the Germans but were under strict instructions to lie low and the girls made sure we did so. You can probably imagine what it was like, two boys and two girls, things, well, happened between us. James and Aimee were especially close, they were older and soon hit it off together. Claire spent all her time trying to stop me going out and shooting the first German I met but yes, we became lovers. It was a special time for the four of us; with the knowledge that victory was close we didn't want to mess things up, so kept a low profile. We knew we would have our revenge soon.

'The girls showed us around the local area, the four of us were never together outside, one couple would always watch the other from a safe distance. We were unarmed, strict orders from Paul. There were hardly any Germans about, occasionally we saw the odd staff car driving past but the city seemed devoid of the enemy. A few days later we received a message saying that strikes would commence on the transport system, in the postal service and on the docks. This was the prelude to the uprising, meaning the Allies were close. The orders also stated that if the enemy began to destroy the city and kill the population we should begin the uprising without waiting for further orders. The girls went out and collected what food they could and came back saying they had heard French and English radio broadcasts in a café saying that liberation was now close. The strikes paralysed the city but the Germans did nothing but leave their apartments, offices and barracks, heading east, defeated. Aimee and Claire were convinced that the Nazis were terrified of French retribution so were slipping away quietly and for the same reason, would not destroy the city. Two days later the order came through to start the rising.

'James and myself would help build and man a barricade at the eastern end of the Boulevard Saint-Germain. The girls were to go to a nearby church and take sheets with them to cut up for bandages and help with the wounded. They told us that they wouldn't do it, that they would be with us at the barricade and die with us, just like the women of Paris had always done. Aimee was crying, Claire threw her arms around me saying she would never leave me.

'It was James who took control, dabbing away Aimee's tears. He spoke in his broken French to the three of us. He told us that France had suffered terribly for the past four years but was now on the verge of victory. It was important for them to survive the battle and rebuild the country for coming generations. He said that they were all young and had their life ahead of them, they would go onto have children and they could tell their children how they had defeated a hideous enemy, against all odds. He told the girls that they were needed by their comrades at the church, that their work was vitally important to the success of the battle and their ancestors would be proud of them. Finally, he told us that as an Englishman he was incredibly honoured to have fought alongside French men and women for the past two years and that France would be in his blood, forever.

'Aimee threw her arms around him saying they would all go to the church together and the boys would then go to the barricade to fight. Fifteen minutes later the girls had changed into pants, boots and old army shirts they had cut down to fit. Claire brought a haversack full of tricolour armbands from under a bed and we pinned one to each other's sleeve. James brought in the Sten guns, pistols and ammunition and checked the magazines. He handed a pistol to each girl and smiled. They had cleaned the weapons with their sewing machine oil and we had shown them how to shoot them. Together we set off for the church, four uniformed and armed soldiers ready to liberate their country.

'The streets were full of fighters like ourselves all hurrying to rendezvous points. Some tricolours were being flown from windows and in the distance, we could hear the odd shot being fired. Some old people and children came to their doors to wish us luck but we told them to go back inside and stay safe. We kept to the building line half-running, half-walking, James in front with his Sten, the kitbag tied to his back with rope. The girls were between us holding their pistols, their haversacks packed with supplies. I brought up the rear scanning around to make sure no one attacked from the back. A car drove by at a fast speed with "FFI" painted on the side and a tricolour flying from the back.

'The church was a kind of command post with fighters coming and going. Aimee and Claire emptied their bags of armbands, sheets and bandages onto a table as the man known as "Paul" walked through the front door. He immediately began to give out orders to everyone in a calm, measured way. When he reached James and myself he took us to where a map of the city had been laid out on a table. Several of us gathered around to listen. He explained that Free French armoured forces under General Leclerc had reached the western outskirts of the city but the Germans were expected to counter attack at any time and we must stop them wherever they may appear. In our sector, we were to stop any movement across the Jardin du Luxembourg and along the Boulevard Saint-Germain towards the city centre. He told James and myself he wanted us to take charge of one of the main barricades in that area. He had just come from there and said that it was being constructed by teenagers and women and although they were doing a great job they needed experienced soldiers with them. We found the girls who were busy pinning armbands on everyone and told them we were leaving. They were strong now, they hugged and kissed us saying they would see us back at the shop when the battle was over.

'When we reached the Boulevard Saint-Germain the barricade was almost built. Dozens of civilians were piling on sand, paving stones and bags of grain to reinforce it. Some youths about my own age had old rifles, swords and bayonets and were waving them in the air. We were shocked, we both knew these people would be wiped out should the Germans attack. Paul had promised us some more fighters as soon as they became available but till then we would have to make do. We gathered everyone together, told the women to go and fill bottles of water and bring some food. We had stuffed our pockets with tricolour armbands and began to distribute them. Some other fighters arrived from the church armed with Stens and captured German rifles, haversacks stuffed with ammunition and bandages. Two others carried a crate of old wine bottles filled with petrol and rags that we could light and throw, you know, Molotov cocktails. James took charge, putting an armed fighter with each group of teenagers and tried to get some sort of order into things. He climbed to the top of the fortification and looked through his binoculars towards the Luxembourg gardens. He came down, called me over and said that he could see some men in German uniforms, some without uniform carrying rifles. If they stayed where they were they could not harm us but if they moved into the high buildings in front of us they could be a real danger firing from above. We got everyone as close to the back of the barricade as possible, the women distributed water and bread and we waited.

'Our main worry was if the enemy used tanks and artillery we would be blown away. James told his section leaders that if that happened we should retreat to the buildings and throw the petrol bombs from height at the tanks. As the day wore on it got hotter and we could hear some sporadic shooting in the distance but nothing seemed to be happening near us. Our old friends, the crew of the barge arrived to help, the captain resplendent in his tunic and medals, a huge revolver in a holster at his waist. Claire came from the church with a bag of ammunition, armbands, bandages and a small tin that she gave to me telling me it was morphine. Claire told us that Aimee was helping Paul and the others in the church and that fighting had started north of the river. I hugged her and told her to stay safe before she left to return to the command post. Ten minutes later two teenagers climbed onto the barricade and looked over. Immediately, one was shot in the head, the other in the shoulder. James shouted for everyone to stay down as he looked between two grain sacks on top of the barricade. Another shot flew over his head into the roadway behind us. He reached down to me for his binoculars and said "Snipers. Tell everyone to stay tucked into the barricade and don't do anything until I say". He scanned the buildings in front of us for several minutes as our medics worked on the boy's shoulder. I opened the tin Claire had given me and passed a full hypodermic down the line. The other boy was dead, covered with his jacket, lying on the roadway.

'James climbed down and called his section leaders to him. He told us that we needed to draw their fire so we could locate their positions. He grabbed a beret off one of them and told them to wait for orders. I had to hold the hat on a stick whilst he watched the apartment blocks to our left. Several shots rang out and we looked behind. A woman with her two children had been shot as they walked along the building line, bringing us bread. One of our boys ran to her aid and was also shot. It all happened so fast, all our fighters jumped up and began firing away at the buildings. It was chaos. Two fighters fell back, dead. The barge captain was firing his long pistol at a window and shouting to James, "I see them!" James was shouting for everyone to get down as we went along the line pulling them down by their legs to safety.

'The captain showed James where he had seen the shots coming from and he quickly gathered myself and two of Paul's men to him. He told us we had to act quickly before the enemy moved position. James, myself and another would get through the barricade where it met the building line, a small gap had been left for this purpose. One was to stay and respond to our hand signals for covering fire, three of us would make to a deep doorway about 50 metres away which would give us a better angle of fire at the sniper's position across the street. The three of us ran for the doorway whilst all our fighters fired on the sniper's position. We made it and James took the German rifle from our comrade, handing him his Sten. The plan was for the two of us to draw the sniper's fire using our Stens while James would take him with the rifle. We got into position, identified the window and opened fire as he came into view. James fired two shots with the rifle and then silence. We had to wait. After 15 minutes, we gave the hand signal for the barricade to try the beret trick again. Nothing happened. We waited another five minutes and gave the signal for the fighters to gives us cover fire. As they opened up we made a dash for the gap in the barricade. Our comrade went first, I was in the middle, James made up the rear.'

Jean-Michel was looking at the table and had stopped talking. He was shaking his head very slightly then slowly looked at Mike. A train had just arrived and the Frenchman said quietly, 'That's her train.' Mike looked round at the train, bemused, but Jean continued.

'It all happened so fast. Our comrade got through the gap and I looked up to see our brave men and women on top of the barricade shouting and pointing to something behind me. I looked back and saw James on the ground. I ran back, grabbed his shirt collar to drag him towards safety. He was too heavy so I pulled him into the nearest doorway and propped him against the wall. His eyes rolled to the back of his head as I ripped open the bloodstained front of his shirt. Much of his insides fell into my hands and I just started crying; for the first time in two years I didn't know what to do, so I did what I had always done, I asked him. He said just two words before he died, "Tell Aimee".'

Mike looked down at the table and said nothing. Hearing voices he looked up and saw Jean-Michel speaking in French to a woman dressed in a rail-workers uniform. She looked from man to man before Jean-Michel smiled and said to Mike, 'This is my wife Claire, I think you may have met her, a long time ago.'

Claire went into the café to ring Veronique to tell her Mike was leaving and would be at the hotel in around 20 minutes. Jean-Michel walked with him to the Metro escalator and they shook hands. The bus driver gave him a piece of paper with the location of James's grave.

'You will find it Michael, it's the only one in English amongst all the French ones.'

Mike put it in his pocket and said, 'What was he like... James?'

As he turned to walk away Jean-Michel stopped and looked at Mike.

'He was just like you my friend.'

49

Chapter 4

Mike felt a hand rubbing his shoulder. 'Dad, Dad, wake up, it's almost one-thirty in the morning, what are you doing sleeping down here?' It was Georgie who had come home after her night out.

'I'm just making some coffee; do you want one?' Georgie could drink coffee anytime of the day or night. She disappeared and returned with two cups.

'Sorry love, I was well away, dreaming about Paris.'

'Was that when you were a student there, Dad?'

Mike grinned, 'Hardly Georgie, I was only there for a few days, but I did go back a few times when I first started teaching, it's a very special place, especially the first time.'

'Matt and I are thinking of going in the summer after my A Levels. Why don't you tell me what it was like when you where there all those years ago?'

Mike smiled, told her he liked Matt and she should bring him around to meet Mum and Sam sometime. He then told her something of Paris in 1979...

The next morning Mike went down to breakfast in a small room just off the tiny reception area. He was met by Veronique who showed him to a small table covered by a gingham tablecloth, a vase of fresh flowers stood at the centre. He sat down and she brought over a pot of coffee and a small jug of milk. He had met her last night when he arrived, a pleasant middle-aged woman who could speak only a little English. She pointed out a large table filled with food and indicated that he should help himself. The food, though simple was wonderful with all kinds of cooked meats, hard boiled eggs, cheeses, croissants and bread. Presently, a heavy-set man in a long apron who was obviously the cook brought out a plateful of steaming hot sausages to Mike's table. There was the usual greeting of '*Bonjour Monsieur*' before he swept back to the kitchen only to return with more sausages for another guest.

After breakfast Mike gathered his camera, sunglasses, map and guidebook, put them in his small shoulder bag and headed off eastwards down the Boulevard Saint-Germain. He cut up the side streets near Odeon heading for the river. At a small stationary shop, he bought a hard-backed notebook and a couple of pens which he popped into his bag. At Notre Dame, he took a few photographs outside the cathedral before crossing onto the north bank near Hotel de Ville and heading west along the Rue de Rivoli, his first stop was to be the Louvre.

Mike sat in the small café on the Rue de Saint-Roch, ordered his lunch, opened his bag and took out the notebook to write. Before he began he thought about the Louvre. For the past three hours, he had wandered around the most amazing building he had ever been in. Glancing at his plan it was clear that he had only seen a fraction of the collection, it would take three days, or weeks to see it all. He had seen the *Mona Lisa* and probably like many others, been underwhelmed. He much preferred Leonardo's *La belle ferronnière*. It was Romanticism that had impressed him most, David, Delacroix, Gericault and the German, Friedrich. There was one painting that stuck in his mind, Eugene Delacroix's *Liberty Leading the People.* He looked at a postcard of the work he had bought in the gift shop. After sustaining casualties at the barricade the defenders looked to an inspirational figure to lead them to onwards to victory. They then charge forward to win the day. A brilliant piece of iconic pro-paganda, a timeless symbol of the Romantic era; as relevant now as then, or for that matter, in August 1944. He opened the notebook and wrote:

'The Barricade, 1944'

After lunch, he went into the Jardin de Tuileries, a haven for occasional lovers, readers and sunbathers. He sat on one of the cream-coloured metal chairs with the Louvre buildings on his right, his face turned towards the sun's warmth, his eyes closed. How long had he been in Paris? Not yet 24 hours, yet it seemed a week at least. The city was beautiful, there was absolutely no question about that, an architectural masterclass. A metropolis that gave the impression of spaciousness despite being one of the most densely populated cities on earth. He could hear a girl's voice somewhere close, chatting and laughing, then a man, more serious, yet encouraging and sensual. Lovers? Possibly, probably. The language was like liquid gold, flowing, expressive and attractive, a feast for the ears. He could make out a few words and phrases but decided to have a look. The girl was perched seductively on one of the chairs about ten metres away. She leaned back and threw one of her legs in the air, laughing at the man who was busily taking photographs of her, a backdrop of fountains against the Louvre made it the perfect location. Occasionally the photographer would move in close to picture her face, she reacted by pouting and smiling into the camera. Occasionally, he would lean over and kiss her on the cheek, whispering a few words into her ear which would bring about a smile, or occasionally, a questioning look from the girl. Mike wondered if they were professionals in their respective roles. The photographer had placed his camera bag and tripod on the ground and was using a large camera with a motor drive. She was tall, beautiful, and posed like she had done this hundreds of times. Finally, the photographer walked to her, bent over and kissed her fully on the mouth putting his hand on the side of her face before moving it down onto her breast. They broke away, he packed away his gear, she picked up her jacket and they walked off past him as if he wasn't there.

He walked through the gardens to the Jeu de Paume to see the Impressionists. Originally built as a conservatory, the building was converted into tennis courts by Napoleon III. Since 1947 it had housed the greatest collection of Impressionist paintings under one roof. He drifted through the long thin structure taking in each painting from the early works of Manet, Degas and Monet to the late or post-Impressionists, Van Gogh, Cezanne and Gauguin. The very nature of colour and light had been explored and dissected and put together again into the first art movement of the modern age.

He stopped for some time at the famous self-portrait by Van Gogh, the one where his eyes appear to follow you wherever you move to. Only two colours dominate, grey and the rust red of his beard. Did the swirls of grey floating around him and blending with his clothes represent the turmoil of his mind? His deep frown appeared to be a warning not to approach, that he was desperately trying to work things out and it might be better if he was left alone. A year later he would be dead. Mike had earlier passed a self-portrait of Paul Gauguin and he went back to it knowing the turbulent, yet fruitful relationship between the two artists.

Gauguin, the classic bohemian, who rejected bourgeois society to dedicate his life to art stares at the watcher with a mocking confidence, the background dominated by his favourite colour, green, and one of his Tahitian girls lying dead on a bed. He wears his hat jauntily, his Breton jumper and coat as if ready to go outside of this special, intimate space. A diagonal flash of yellow sunlight cuts across the wall behind him, perhaps pushing him and his art into another century, one that would be more appreciative, more understanding: yet Gauguin with his world-weary gaze also appears to warn us that the future will be harsher, deadlier, horribly destructive of all things beautiful and simple. The first Impressionists had documented the rise of industry, mass-production, transport and consumerism. Their late followers, Cezanne, Van Gogh and Gauguin had looked for a simpler, more primitive art to express what they could see coming, a twentieth century dominated by hatred, death and destruction with a new type of art they had pioneered.

He wandered out into the gardens and sat on a stone bench still thinking about the most amazing art collection he had ever seen. From somewhere close by he could hear a drum banging and a megaphone. The sound was coming from his left, out on the street. He walked to the nearby railings and looked out onto the Place de la Concorde where thousands of people were forming up into lines and starting to move off towards the Rue de Rivoli. He went through a gate to the street just as the first marchers reached him. The front line took up the entire roadway and carried a long banner in front of them, Mike just catching the words '*Non*' and 'Éducation' on the banner before they passed him. The marchers were chanting, some were blowing whistles and the drum was banging somewhere towards the rear. As the fourth row reached him an arm reached out to his pulling at his sleeve and then linking his arm as he involuntarily joined the march.

It was a girl. She looked ahead, chanting some sort of slogan together with the crowd. She had dark hair tied in a pony-tail. She was petit and wore a blue denim shirt and white trousers with blue plimsoles. Most of the marchers were about his own age with the occasional older person sprinkled in and linking arms with the younger ones. She turned and they looked at each other. She said something in French to him which was drowned out by the noise. He gestured with his hand to his ear, leaning towards her. This time she shouted but he could only understand one or two words, one being 'university'. He shrugged and asked her if she spoke English. She looked at him quizzingly, loosening her grip on his arm a little and said in English.

'OK, what college are you studying at in Paris?'

'I'm not from Paris, I'm at university in England.'

She smiled and said, 'Well OK, welcome to a French student demonstration. It's against the Government who are trying to cut funding to universities.'

As they looked at each other Mike thought she looked just like one of the girl's in Renoir's *Le Moulin de la Gallette*. He had been looking at the painting just half an hour earlier.

They sat in the café together, Mike drinking a beer, her name was Suzanne and she sipped a long glass of Ricard topped with water. She was 24 and a student in Paris studying law. They smoked her Gitanes as she told him she was delighted that he had stayed with the march all the way to the Place de la Republique and even stayed to listen to the speakers. She spoke good English, if heavily accented.

'Did you hear the reception that de Beauvoir got when she stood up to speak? She's a little uneasy on her feet these days but still has her marvellous mind. A pity Sartre could not be there but he is very weak and almost blind these days.'

Mike looked at her, he had heard of Sartre but not de Beauvoir. 'I presume she's very important.'

Suzanne flicked her cigarette into the ashtray and told him about Simone de Beauvoir and how important she was to the feminist movement and existentialism.

'Anyway, I'm sure you know about all that, now tell me, have you seen Paris by night?'

'No, I only arrived yesterday, I'm still finding my way around.'

She paused leaning towards him, her large brown eyes fixed on his.

'Well Michael, perhaps you will let me show you my city.'

They went back to her apartment where she lived with her parents which was in a wealthy area around 15 minutes' walk from the café. She acknowledged the concierge as they entered and went up three floors in one of those old-fashioned iron lifts with caged sides. The apartment had huge double mahogany doors that she unlocked and pushed open with her shoulder. Suzanne showed him into a large room that was a kind of cross between a library and lounge telling him to make himself at home before she disappeared. Mike looked around at the wooden panelling, the book cases and Chesterfield settees. There was wealth here, old, influential wealth. French windows led onto a balcony, the whole place was like a film set from the nineteenth century. Mike looked at the books, many leather bound, Hugo, Balzac, Dumas, Stendhal, Sand, Proust and Zola amongst hundreds of others. A clock ticked quietly on a marble mantelpiece as he made himself comfortable in one of the Chesterfields. He picked up a fashion magazine from a small pile on a glass coffee table and leafed through the pages.

Just over ten minutes later she returned and he was taken completely by surprise. She stood in front of the fireplace brushing her hair in the mirror. She wore a white silk blouse, black pleated calf length skirt and black high heels. Her hair was now a fashionable page-boy style and she turned to him, lit two cigarettes with a marble lighter, placing one between his lips. As she leaned over he smelt Chanel No 5. She looked ravishing.

'I won't be long, almost ready,' she said as she left the room again.

Mike wasn't often speechless but didn't quite know what to say, anyway, he was quite happy to let her speak, she obviously had some sort of plan for the evening. He hoped it wouldn't be anything too expensive.

Suzanne returned and went to the mirror fastening a black velvet choker around her neck. She turned to take her cigarette from the ashtray and muttered something to herself in French. Without even looking at Mike who was facing her she put one foot on the coffee table, lifted her skirt and fastened her suspender to her stocking top which had come undone. She brushed down her skirt, threw her head back and said, 'Ready.'

In the spacious entrance hall, she told him to leave his bag, he could pick it up later. She then rummaged in a small cupboard and found a silk maroon polka-dot scarf which she tied around his neck, smiled and said that now he looked like a real Parisian student.

They ate dinner at a restaurant near the Place de Vosges, Suzanne insisting she would pay as she was the daughter of a banker and he was a poor student. She had three older brothers, one a lawyer, another an army officer and the youngest, a film director. Her parents were spending the summer at their villa in the south of France. After leaving school she had travelled around Europe for a couple of years living in Rome, Vienna and for a while, London. Her first love was art and fashion but her father refused to pay for an art degree so she ended up studying law, something she had little taste for. She was delighted to hear that he was from a working-class background stating that she wished France would give their own working classes the same opportunities as the English do. After the food, they got on to politics and found they were on common ground.

'So, your country has a woman leader for the first time, not a friend of the workers, I believe.'

'Its early days yet, but things were looking bad in the country, no wonder people voted for a change, although I never voted for her. Some have even compared her to your General de Gaulle.'

'Then God help the people of Britain. The sooner France puts his outdated nonsense behind her and moves forward, the better. The man was virtually a dictator, your people would do well to remember that.'

Mike smiled. 'You're not a supporter then?'

'I have a father and two brothers who are Gaullists. Papa was a friend of the man, even helping him politically and financially. De Gaulle should have gone in 1968 when the people rose up but the students were too elitist, they should have made common ground with the workers to overthrow the regime.'

Mike smiled again, lit a Gitanes for them both and said. 'I think the general's supporters across France, especially the working class, had something to do with the failure of that particular revolution.'

She smiled, blew away cigarette smoke, leaned across the table just a few inches from his face and said quietly. 'For a young man, you are very well informed about France, perhaps you should give me some lessons sometime.' She ran her tongue across her upper lip, smiled and took a sip of coffee.

Miked smiled, trying to ignore the obvious sexual innuendo but secretly delighted. He was enjoying himself and continued the discussion:

'Surely his place in history is assured as a war leader and afterwards with the creation of the Common Market. It has led to peace and prosperity for both France and Germany and might do the same for us.'

'Mike, that's a typical English attitude. You always interfere on the mainland of Europe in the wrong way and I give de Gaulle some credit because he was right about that, at least. For years, he stopped your President Wilson joining Europe because he said that Britain would wreck the project. De Gaulle was politically destroyed after May '68, it was others who pushed for and allowed your country to come in, including the Americans who wanted a stronger, capitalist Europe, along their own lines. Britain will always look across the Atlantic and put the Americans before us or for that matter, the Germans or anyone else in Europe.'

He laughed a little, 'Prime minister Suzanne... Harold Wilson

57

was our prime minister. You're getting mixed up with Woodrow Wilson, the American president.'

She smiled and said, 'Another Anglo-Saxon who screwed up my country.'

They both laughed at the joke. He slipped his hand across the table onto the back of her hand. She smiled knowingly, called the waiter, took his hand and said, 'Enough of politics, come on, lets enjoy ourselves.'

Mike sat down on one of the rickety chairs pulling his sweat soaked shirt away from his chest and reached for a cigarette. He had just danced very closely with the most beautiful girl he had ever seen who had pushed her body into his to some sort of slow, sultry jazz tune. He had envisioned a jazz club to be filled with middle-aged men in baggy jumpers and duffel coats, yet here everyone seemed to be under 25 and looked the coolest people on the planet. The band had sped up again and he watched Suzanne dancing with a man in the centre of the small dance floor. She was a superb dancer and he had felt completely inadequate when dancing with her earlier in the evening. The other dancers parted in appreciation leaving the floor to the couple to gyrate, rock and jive to the pounding music. The band played a mixture of jazz, rock, rhythm and blues and pop with bags of saxophone, guitar, bass, drums, keyboard and a brilliant trumpeter who now stepped forward with a piercing solo to Santana's 'Black Magic Woman'. As they finished the whole club gave the band and the two dancers a standing ovation.

Suzanne came back to the table as Mike was still standing, applauding. She gave him a mock bow and smiled before taking a cigarette. Mike poured two glasses of red wine, handed one to her and said, 'Well done, you missed your calling.' She moved her chair closer to his and leaned her face towards his so they could talk above the noise.

'So how do you like the club?'

'Its... fabulous, not what I expected, much, much better. I like the resident dancers, especially the girl.' She moved a little closer, laughing and saying, 'You were doing pretty well yourself out there, dancing with Sophie.'

'You know her?'

'Yes of course, we're students together, it's a good job I'm not the jealous type, she could make Bardot look plain.' She grabbed his hand and half pulled him towards the dance-floor putting her arms around his neck as the band struck up 'Baker Street'. Their cheeks met and she whispered that she loved this song when she lived in England. The saxophone solo cut through the air, she looked at him and said, 'I'm a complete Anglophile, especially tonight.'

He couldn't make out what was lying across his face. He felt terrible but wasn't yet conscious enough to understand that that he had a hangover. Everything was too bright, too white. It was at this point that he realised he was lying on his back and yes, it was a hangover. The thing across his face was hard and soft and had red bits. He reached up and with some difficulty lifted it up whereby it came in visual focus. A hand, a girl's hand, with red nail polish. Then he realised who the girl was and started to recall last night. He placed the hand down, turned over and saw her, muttering something in her sleep. He managed to make it to the bathroom, more out of instinct than from finding it last night. He stood at the sink looking in the mirror trying to summon up courage to swill his face when she came in putting her arms around his waist from behind. They stood there for a few seconds motionless, naked, propping each other up. She mumbled something in French and moved a hand down towards his genitals. Mike shook his head, smiled at her in the mirror and said, 'Suzanne... It's impossible.' She giggled and said, 'I know... coffee?'

They had breakfasted on coffee, orange juice and aspirin at a huge wooden table in the kitchen. Suzanne told him that next year the deeds of the apartment would be hers. Her brothers all had their own houses, her father had retired and her parents would move permanently to the south this winter. She joked that she would still be in the place, by herself, in 50 years hence, an aged spinster still going on marches and putting the world to right. They showered together and she found a gold razor, shaving brush and some soap in a marble dish for him to shave. When he returned to the kitchen she was ironing his shirt and looked radiant, her hair back in the pony tail wearing a pristine white shirt and jeans. He moved behind her putting his hands around her waist, gently kissing her neck. He got the desired reaction but she said, 'No… later, today, you see Paris by day.'

It turned out to be unforgettable. The Picasso Museum, the Pompidou Centre, Napoleon's Tomb and the Eiffel Tower. They finished off the day at the Pantheon and as they came down the steps she suggested he walk along to his hotel, pay his bill and pick up his bag. He could stay at the apartment.

Two days later she accompanied him to the Gare de l'Est to catch the bus to Calais. They had been silent on the Metro and as they came out onto the station concourse he checked the clock. They had around ten minutes before the bus left. They walked to a quiet corner where he put his rucksack on the ground. He was fidgety and silent as he lit a cigarette. She leaned against a wall, held out her hands and said, 'Mike come here.' She held him close, looking up into his eyes. He realised for the first time how small she was, perhaps five foot two, no more.

'Mike, the past few days have been wonderful for both of us. You have been and will always be, very special to me.'

He went to speak but she put a gentle finger on his lips. He let her speak, she was older, wiser, the dominant partner. She would know how to handle this parting.

'My other lovers have all been older men who have only wanted me for sex or as a potential wife from a wealthy family. They were all totally selfish. You are different, young, happy and giving. For the first time in my life a man has put me first in everything we have done together. You have made me happier than I have ever been and I will admit something to you, I am a little bit in love.'

He realised that she most likely meant it, her English had become more accented as she spoke, something he had noticed each time she spoke passionately about something.

'I want you to know Mike that I will always be here for you. When you return to Paris you know where I will be, always come and see me.' She was smiling now. 'It doesn't matter if you have a wife and kids in tow, we will always be friends, forever. Nations, flags, countries, borders, they don't matter. The only thing that matters in life are people. Remember, it's not what you leave behind, it's what you take with you that counts.' She kissed him tenderly and they parted.

When he returned home and unpacked his rucksack he found a leather-bound book like the ones on the shelves in the apartment's library. It was by Jean-Paul Sartre and in French. As he opened it an envelope fell out. It contained a long, handwritten letter and a lock of her dark hair tied with blue ribbon. Two years later Mike returned to Paris, his first stop was a small cemetery wedged between two apartment blocks just south of the Jardin de Luxembourg. A tricolour flew in the centre of the graveyard which held about 30 graves. In a corner, he found a grey headstone with a simple inscription in English.

James Rayner
A Soldier of France
August 1944

Georgie had slumped against his shoulder as he was talking but when he finished she said, 'Dad, that was amazing, what was she like, that girl, Suzanne. I bet she was dead pretty, French girls usually are, I remember when we went on the school trip in Year 11, the boys couldn't believe their luck when they saw the girls.'

'Well, she was more attractive than pretty, stylish, clever, just very... French. Anyway young lady, God knows what time of night it is and I for one have had an exhausting day. As for Paris, I'm sure you and Matt will love the place, just as I did.'

Chapter 5
September 2016

The first few days back at school after the summer term are always busy. To make things run as smoothly as possible the staff come back for two days before the pupils. After Rachel had addressed everyone in the hall each subject department went their separate ways to discuss staff responsibilities and duties. The art department had been boosted by an extra member of staff, arranged just before they broke for the summer. Kirsty, their student who had now qualified as a teacher had been offered a contract to work alongside Angie and Mike. She was to take over some of Mike's classes as the headteacher had something else in mind for him. Kirsty made three cups of coffee and they sat around their tiny departmental staff room which was nothing more than a converted storeroom.

'The Head Girl wants to see us both at eleven Mike,' said Angie.

'Oh, joy. I can't wait. Perhaps she's going to make me a deputy head or maybe offer me an attachment to the Department of Education.'

Kirsty said, 'You're famous now Mike, my Mum saw you on the TV after the Referendum.'

All three laughed and Angie said, 'A daytime TV star Mike, the world's your oyster now.'

There was more laughter before the conversation turned to Brexit. It was Angie who brought things back to earth.

'I've been home over the summer. People are worried about Brexit. Nobody, except one or two idiots on both sides wants a return to the Troubles. Talk of border controls and customs posts is a genuine concern. The power-sharing agreement is fragile enough without this as well.'

Mike looked at Kirsty and said in a serious voice. 'Do you know what Angie means by the Troubles in Northern Ireland Kirsty?'

'Yes, we learnt something about it at school, and at uni I roomed up with a girl from Belfast for the first year. That's not going to happen again, is it? I thought it was all sorted now Angie.'

'I'm afraid over there sweetie the old problems never really go away, they just lie low waiting for a spark to set them off again. Let's hope this new government we've got now keeps an eye on things although I fear they will have their hands full over this Brexit business.' Mike decided the subject needed changing and spoke to Kirsty about what classes of his she would be taking on. Angie took the hint and started to go through the timetables for the new Year 7s.

Mike took his coffee into the empty classroom thinking about the summer, which had passed too quickly. Georgie had her A Level results and received a few offers to study art from universities around the country. After much deliberation, she decided to stay at home and go to Liverpool. This wasn't entirely surprising to Mike, knowing about her relationship with Matt. He was generally indifferent but Jane seemed annoyed that she wouldn't be going away. Jane had left home at 18, gone to university at the other end of the country and felt it had done her no harm whatsoever. Eventually, mother and daughter came to a compromise of sorts. Georgie would spend the first year at home and then consider moving into other accommodation. Having two women in the house was starting to prove difficult; they were at opposite ends of the emotional spectrum. Sam, like a favourite pet, simply went off into gaming land when things heated up between his mother and sister.

Matt had come for dinner before he went home for the summer. Everything had gone well and Jane, a fellow southerner, had found much common ground with him, chatting away as if she'd known him for years. They talked about his upbringing in the south of England, his parents and the places they both knew well. Jane told him that she didn't get home enough these days with work and raising a family and that he was fortunate to be able to visit his parents during the holidays. To Mike, it seemed simple friendliness but as the night went on he watched Georgie's face and knew that she was becoming a little jealous. He also knew that Georgie would have it fixed in her mind that her mother was behaving the way she was to deliberately upset her. At the end of the night as Matt was leaving Jane put her arms around him, kissing his cheek, telling him to call anytime he was passing, Georgie hardly got a look in and flew up the stairs in rage as the door closed behind Matt.

Things came to head a few days later when Jane was kept late at school, Sam had gone off to play football with some friends and Mike was sitting in the kitchen with Georgie.

'Not seeing Matt tonight George?'

She didn't look up from her phone straight away and then said quietly, 'He's busy getting all his work done before he goes home, it's a tough course Dad, veterinary.'

'I can imagine it is, did he enjoy himself the other night?'

Georgie put her phone down and turned to face him, folding her arms. Mike realised he'd said the wrong thing.

'I've no doubt he had a lovely time chatting with mum, all they did was go on about how wonderful it was in Surrey, Essex and so on.'

'Oh, come on George, Mum doesn't get to see her family much these days, it must have been nice for her to meet someone from her neck of the woods and Matt seemed to be delighted.'

'What's that supposed to mean? He's going out with me, not her. She was overdoing the whole thing Dad, simply to make me jealous. This is her home, she's been here for thirty years, she behaved the way she did just to upset me.'

'Oh, come on Georgie, your mum loves you, she wouldn't do that. Look, I think you're overreacting a bit. Your mum is attractive for her age, most 23-year-old men would be charmed by her. Please, let's call a truce on this one, it would really please me to see both of you make things up.'

'I'm sorry Dad, I never meant to hurt you, it's not your fault. I might have overreacted a bit. It's not Matt's fault either, I suppose I've been a bit unfair on him as well.' She started to smile and said,

'Matt even said I got my looks from mum. I suppose she is a bit of a looker, I just hope I look that good at her age.'

'I'll make you a coffee for a change Georgie and we'll go and watch the news together.'

Later that evening Mike was catching up with some work when Sam, showered and changed after the football came and sat in the room with him.

'Dad, we've been doing some things in history which some people think could be repeating themselves because of Brexit.'

Mike closed his laptop and asked what subjects they had been studying.

'The problems in Europe after the First World War. We've been looking at the Versailles Treaty, the Weimar Republic in Germany, the rise of the Nazis and the collapse of the League of Nations. Could Brexit be like those things, which eventually led to World War Two?'

Mike put his laptop on the floor. Sam was a serious, sensitive boy and had asked a good question.

'No, I don't think Brexit by itself could lead to anything like that. For instance, we now know that the Versailles Treaty was too heavy on Germany and it handed Hitler a propaganda victory with the German people, enabling him to win power. The Weimar Republic failed to rebuild the country's economy and let down the working classes, who then turned towards extremism on both the right and left. The League of Nations was always seen as an Anglo-Saxon club that would only look after The United States and Britain. France and Italy, who were on the Allied side during the war, felt that it didn't address their interests. Mussolini was particularly scathing about it, with some justification; and don't forget about Russia, or the Soviet Union as it was then called. The other countries were worried about the threat, real or perceived, from them. All these ingredients, and many others led to war in 1939.'

Mike rose to his feet, went over and tapped Sam on the head, leaving the room before his son could reply. He walked into the kitchen, poured himself a glass of water and sat down. He had taken the easy way out with Sam and left the room. Brexit by itself probably couldn't lead to a melt-down but together with other problems around the world and a worry that it would have a knock-on effect in the United States and Europe was a big concern of Mike's. However, now it was very much a what-if situation and currently Brexit was looked upon by many countries as a typical English farce and muddle. Only time could answer Sam's question.

Angie came into the classroom saying it was time for their 11 o'clock appointment with Rachel. There was nothing unusual about these meetings at the start of a new term, all the department heads and deputies would be seeing the head in half-hour slots throughout the day. Once they had been through the summer exam results Rachel settled back in her seat with her pleased look.

'Well you two, another fine year, well done. I know that you will both help Kirsty along. Mike, I mentioned before we broke up that I had some plans for you and that Kirsty would be taking over some of your classes. You will still be doing A Level and some Year 10 and 11 classes but I want you to put something together so the school can start teaching politics from next year, hopefully at GCSE and A Level.' Rachel put her hands up in a slightly defensive posture and continued speaking. 'I think it's very important in the age we live in for young people to know how our political system works. A lot of these problems we're having across the country over Brexit are down to the fact that people simply aren't informed enough.'

As she spoke Mike noticed that every now and then she glanced at notes on her desk. He wondered who had put these ideas in her head. Guy Simpson? Maybe, but Guy would only do that if there was something in it for him. He agreed with Rachel about the fact that most people didn't understand how the system works and the problems would only get worse as the new Government went about the process of Brexit. There were court cases in the pipeline that would add to the complicated process and he doubted that the average voter, whatever side they were on in last June's Referendum would be able to get their head around most of it.

'I'm giving you the time Mike to get out on the ground and

speak to people. Go and see our local MP, that chap who came on a visit to the school early last year. I suggest you visit parliament and while you're there make an appointment to see someone from the Department of Education, they have lots of young men and women who would be only too happy to add the assistance they gave to us to their personal CV. See what other schools do, there's a local independent school who have excellent politics results every year, I'll call the headteacher and see if you can pop round.'

Angie intervened. 'Rachel, wouldn't we be better putting something together about politics and Brexit in PHSE for the kids. I know these things are important but we live in financially difficult times in schools, surely we could get something like that going.'

'Angie, I know you're probably concerned about losing Mike to this. That is why I have taken Kirsty on for you. Mike, if you think we should just start with GCSE then that's fine for the first two years, then we can move to A Level as well. Don't worry, we'll get somebody else in to teach A Level when it comes around. I've left you with Year 10 and 11 art students to give you some time to put something together. I have had have a word with Stefan, he'll arrange for you to speak on Year 8 and 9 assemblies about GCSE politics being a new option.' Rachel stood up and brushed down her skirt with both hands indicating that the interview was at an end.

During the walk back to the art department Angie was shaking her head, saying quietly that Rachel was up to something.

'I know her like the back of my hand Mike, don't forget, I taught her art and history when she was a girl. That thing she does with her skirt, brushing it down with her hands, she did it as a youngster when she was hiding something. I tell you she's got something in mind with all this politics palaver, I'm not sure what exactly it is, no doubt it will all come out eventually.'

'I didn't arrive here until after she had left. What was she like at school?'

'Oh, no problems, she was a bright kid, a pretty girlie who had the boys eating out of her hand. She struggled a little at history and dropped it after her GCSEs, yet still managed a B grade. Excellent at art, one of my best pupils. Went on to do A Level art but sadly, dropped it after the first year. I can't remember exactly what the problem was, some sort of personal or family crisis, poor girl, she had set her heart on becoming an art teacher, I think that's why she has a soft spot for our department. She was off sick for a while and we all thought she may have to leave school. When she returned, it was agreed that she would drop a subject. Unfortunately, it was art.'

Mike had a quiet respect and regard for Rachel Evans. She had done very well for herself despite some sort of setback during her A Levels. The fact that she had managed to get over whatever it was and go on to become a headteacher before she was forty was a major achievement.

That afternoon he popped into his local supermarket on his way home from school. He wandered around picking up a few things, an opportunity to switch off mentally for half an hour. As he manoeuvred his trolley along the meat section two pensioners, probably a married couple, seemed to be having an argument about something. Mike reached across and picked a packet of ham for himself, dropping it into his trolley.

'Hey mate can you tell me what country that meat is from?' The man spoke in a loud voice. Mike thought he might be a little deaf, looked at the packaging and said, 'Germany.'

The man turned to his wife again, 'There we are, what did I tell you, there's no English meat here.'

Mike looked at the man's wife who looked embarrassed.

The man spoke again in a loud voice, 'They've got meat from France, Italy, Ireland and now Germany but no English meat. We're out of Europe now so why have we still got their meat?' He had begun to shout and Mike thought it best to move on but the old man picked up the packet of ham from his trolley and shoved it in front of his face. 'What's going on in this country mate, we voted for Brexit but everything you pick up in this place is foreign.'

A woman in a suit with a badge stating 'Store Manager' said, 'Sir, you have been told before about this behaviour, you must not be abusive to other customers or staff or you will be barred from the store.' Another member of staff arrived and was apologising to Mike. The old couple were ushered away by the staff, Mike feeling very sorry for them. This was one of several incidents he had witnessed over the summer relating to Brexit, and by far the saddest.

Jane had arrived home before him, something of a rarity and both children were out. She kissed him and started to make some tea. Mike sat on a kitchen chair and said to her, 'How's things between you and Georgie these days?'

'Much better now. You know we had a big reconciliation after that silly Matt thing, both blamed ourselves and we ended up hugging each other. Things have been much better since her trip to Paris with Matt, she seems to have matured a lot, it's made her more grown-up somehow, which is good.'

'It's that type of place Jane, makes people grow up very quickly… Perhaps you and I could do with another visit, it might do us good.'

Jane brought the tea over, leant over and kissed him gently on the lips. 'What a good idea, it was brilliant last time, but so long ago, too long.' She nibbled at his ear whispering, '*Je t'aime*, Michel, *Je t'aime* Paris.' He playfully pushed her away laughing and saying, 'Mrs McCarthy, you're a 50-year-old woman, behave yourself!' She sat down still giggling. 'Do you realise Mike, it was almost 30 years ago, I can't believe we haven't been back since. Anyway, its seems to have had a good effect on Georgie which can't be bad. Perhaps we could go sometime next year, I'm sure Mum and Dad would have Sam and we could jump the Eurostar over. The French would be alright with us wouldn't they, you know, about Brexit?'

'Do you know Jane, I've no idea. I can imagine them being pretty pissed-off about it. Traditionally the French don't take too kindly to anyone who has a dig at them, which usually means the English. It's not just about old rivalries, if Brexit damages their economy and leads to extremism, which it could, they won't be happy. The country is essentially conservative so the prospect of change due to something not of their own making will cause problems and they have a general election next year.'

She put her cup down and came and sat on his knee, putting her arms around his neck, laughing and said 'Maybe we should pretend to be Americans.'

'Jane, you and I are the unlikeliest looking Americans on the planet, and besides, that would make it worse.' They both laughed and kissed.

The following week Mike read a newspaper article entitled, 'Post-Truth, How It's Influencing Every Aspect of Our Life.' He was a little bemused by the concept 'Post-Truth.' It seemed to imply that we had always lived in a truthful world or at least a portion of time when truthfulness reigned and it had simply gone away to be replaced by something else, lies perhaps. What had seemed initially one of those frivolous newspaper features used to pad things out when there was little news about became more interesting and relevant as he read on. The article suggested that the phenomenon had been around for a few years, fuelled by social media, unscrupulous journalists, editors and mouthy politicians but had really gained ground during the Referendum campaign. Some examples were given of lurid newspaper headlines, bizarre pronouncements by politicians and so called, expert opinion. Upon further investigation, all the examples given were found to be complete fabrications.

Now there was nothing new about politicians, journalists and experts playing around with the truth, twisting and turning to create a story, getting people to vote for them or trying to gain some sort of advantage. When he was young he had heard his father say, 'Don't believe everything you read in the newspapers.' Surely that still stands today, or are people just more gullible? The author of the piece seemed to be suggesting that this whole business was new. To Mike it had been around since the dawn of time, it didn't matter what format it was put out in. The article concluded with some examples from the current US presidential campaign and a gloomy prognosis that things could only get worse.

Jane was right about Georgie. Following her Paris trip, she appeared calmer, assured and responsible. Perhaps she was just growing up, however, one thing Mike had noticed was she had become more political of late. Again, this could be an age thing or even the influence of Matt and his group of friends, whatever the reason Mike was quietly pleased. It certainly seemed to be keeping the peace between mother and daughter. Georgie was about to start university and her attitude now couldn't be better as far as her parents could see.

There was something else that might be contributing to her changed manner. Before she had left for Paris, Mike had written an address on a piece of paper and asked her to look up an old friend. It hadn't taken Georgie long to realise that the friend living in Paris was Suzanne. Mike had told his daughter Suzanne always welcomed visitors, especially young ones, which was completely true. He had sent a short letter to Suzanne informing her of the visit, she didn't do emails or texts. Upon Georgie's return she told Mike that Suzanne was 'cool, perhaps the coolest person she had ever met.'

Mike spent the next few days contacting the local MP, parliament, the Department of Education and other schools to make appointments with various people. He read over the current politics GCSE curriculum, which he found to be dry, something he would need to address, inside and outside of the classroom to keep the students interested and motivated. Rachel had requested 'fairly regular' meetings with him to keep her abreast of progress. These turned out to be once a week and he found them intriguing. Angie seemed to be correct about one thing, Rachel Evans, if not exactly hiding something, appeared to have some sort of hidden agenda.

It had been a few years since Mike had been to London and it was usually with the family, visiting museums and other tourist attractions. Now he found himself removing his wallet, watch, belt and shoes and placing them along with his briefcase in a large plastic tray which was pushed off into an X-ray machine. He waited in the queue to enter the security archway and looked across to the other side where a young man named Tristram was waiting to meet him. Next to Tristram stood the tallest policeman he had ever seen, holding a black assault rifle. Mike noticed he had his finger on the trigger.

'Welcome to parliament Mr McCarthy, I'm Tristram Clarke, we spoke on the phone.'

They shook hands and walked across a wide, open-plan atrium

towards a café. Tables and chairs were dotted about and the place had the feel of the headquarters of a bank or insurance company. Tristram had gone off to get coffee for them both at an adjacent counter and Mike looked around. This was Portcullis House, as far removed from the average person's idea of England's parliament as it was possible to be. Tristram returned, explaining that the building, newly built, housed the MP's offices, committee rooms and many of the civil servants like himself, who worked day to day in the Mother of all parliaments. Tristram explained that his role was personal assistant to the man Mike had come to see, Nigel Pattison MP.

They were walking around the corridors above the atrium area looking at the paintings of famous politicians, past and present. Tristram had said that Nigel Pattison was currently sitting on the Commons Education Committee and they would go in and listen for a short time. They slid quietly into the back of the modern, green-carpeted Committee room. A woman was giving evidence to the committee about the mental effects that mobile phone use could have on children and young people. She spoke for about ten minutes regarding the dangers of exposure to pornography, gambling and terrorist recruitment sites. For the final five minutes, she warned of the far greater hazards of addiction to the devices, saying that during her research she had found children as young as four and five years of age suffering from serious addiction issues. Mike noticed that for the whole time she was talking a female member of the committee sat looking at her own phone, seemingly oblivious of what was going on around her. The committee chairman invited his members to ask questions of the witness, but none were forthcoming. He thanked the lady, who was a professor at a provincial university for her contribution and adjourned the session until after lunch.

Nigel Pattison came to the back of the room and suggested they all go to the café area to discuss things. Over coffee the MP was effusive about Mike's visit.

'I'm always delighted to have people from schools and colleges from my constituency come down to Westminster, especially as I'm on the Education Committee. When you get going with politics at your school you must bring the pupils here for a visit. I think it's marvellous that your head is doing this, particularly when budgets are tight in schools. You know, I think the more people know about how our political system works, the better for the country as a whole.'

Mike watched him carefully. His body language didn't fit in with his velvet words. He was moving his feet about, looking around and tugging at the sleeve of his suit jacket. Here was a man who wanted to be somewhere else.

'So, would you consider putting down a private member's bill to make it compulsory that politics, including every aspect of our political and constitutional system is taught in schools?'

For a single second Nigel Pattison looked stricken, as if he had been shot. Then much to his credit, he brushed down his lapel, smiled and said, 'I would be in favour of those subjects being taught in schools, however, a PMB now would be almost impossible, I'm afraid Brexit is taking up just about all our parliamentary time.'

Mike replied, 'I understand that you personally campaigned for us to Remain in the EU. There is much evidence to suggest that many voters simply didn't understand what they were voting for, which also includes how parliament itself will be involved in the process. Unfortunately, most people who vote in this country don't have much of an idea how the system works, perhaps if they were educated in school about these matters... In view of that, perhaps you would consider bringing this matter up during one of the many future debates parliament will be holding about how we go about the process of leaving the European Union.'

Pattison had changed his attitude somewhat and now seemed more serious.

'As you can see, Tristram is busy making notes for me. I will address your concerns completely about this Mike and will write to you with details.'

'That's fine, you can always contact me at my school if you require any further information. I think it's a great help having you on the Commons' Education Committee, people at the sharp end in education need as much help as possible from our political representatives.'

Nigel Pattison rose, put out his hand, smiled and said, 'It's been a pleasure to meet you Mike, I'm afraid I have another meeting, perhaps you would like to look around the Palace of Westminster, Tristram knows all the best places and is quite an expert on parliament's history, he would be only too happy to show you around.'

Tristram accompanied Mike around the Palace. They saw Westminster Hall, the lobbies and went upstairs into the Commons' public gallery. Mike had last been here during the 1980s, before TV cameras, before the glass screen had been erected to separate members of parliament from the people who vote for them. They returned to the contemporary glass, aluminium and wood surroundings of Portcullis House and as they said goodbye Mike looked up at the glass roof – for all the world it resembled a bubble.

The following morning, he walked from his hotel to the Department of Education. He was met at the door by a lady called Victoria who held a manila file under her arm. After he had been booked in at reception she took him to an adjacent office where she explained the itinerary for the morning.

'Its most unusual for our teachers to visit the Department, however, you're MP Nigel Pattison contacted us personally to facilitate your visit. It is something we might encourage in the future. I also think it's important that we manage to get out to schools and colleges ourselves more than we do.'

She was the personal assistant to one of the senior Civil Servants in the building and an appointment had been made for Mike to meet him. As she spoke it went through Mike's mind that for some reason they were taking his visit very seriously. He had expected to be taken into an office, given some curriculum guidelines by a junior clerk and sent on his way back to Liverpool. They went up a marvellous old staircase to the second floor where she knocked on an office door with a hand painted sign that read 'Sir George Carter'.

Sir George turned out to be something of a character. Late 60s, bearded and dressed in a bottle-green tweed suit he shook Mike's hand vigorously and ushered him to an easy chair whilst ordering coffee.

'I'm delighted you have come to see us Michael. I know of your headteacher and arranged the Secretary of State's visit to your school three years ago. He was very impressed with the school and Rachel Evans. I also understand that you are something of a television personality, Michael.'

'I wouldn't go that far Sir George, I was thrown into it at the time of the Referendum and since then have taken part in a couple of radio debates, nothing else.'

'Ah that's our friends in the media for you; they'll be all over you while they need you, but tend to drop you like a stone as soon as something else comes along. Having said that, they do have a habit of popping up like a bad penny, just when you're least expecting it. It's a sort of ownership thing with them, once they have you in their clutches they never let go.' He was laughing as he poured out coffee for them both.

The next hour went quickly, they chatted about the school and its plans to teach politics. He was in total agreement with the idea and made some suggestions to Mike to 'lighten the load' for the students. In addition to visiting parliament, he suggested taking them off to the local council chamber, have them meet local and national politicians, get them out on the ground speaking to members of the public about what their level of knowledge of politics is. He kept coming back to Rachel Evans, saying that he was sure that she would be conducive to all these things.

As they spoke Mike couldn't help thinking that he was getting preferential treatment. Why, he had no idea. He kept thinking about what Angie had said about Rachel, that she was hiding something. No, it was probably just the fact that she was a pet headteacher of the Department, one that they could put up as a shining example to other schools and the media, he was simply Rachel's running boy. Yet, he also suspected that the genial Sir George was being economical with the truth. Mike decided to push things a little.

'It's very good of you Sir George to look after me like this, I must tell you it's not what I expected, in fact, I'm not sure what I expected.'

Sir George Carter paused for a moment before he answered.

'I can see that you are perceptive Michael. Let me tell you what I have in mind. We are always looking for schools that are progressive, schools that we can put up as shining beacons of modernity and forward thinking. I know that your school, your headteacher, staff and school community fall into this category. Because of this I'm going to allocate one of my best staff as a point of contact between your school and the Department. He or she will come up to Liverpool to visit the school and your headteacher will have a point of contact, here at the Department. I'm going to write to Rachel with my proposals and suggestions today.' He stood up and put out his hand, indicating that the meeting was over.

Mike returned to Liverpool by train the same afternoon. On the train, he thought about the people he had met over the previous two days. In his view the visit to parliament was mainly a waste of time. His overall impression was of an institution that was outmoded and becoming less relevant to the British people every hour of every day. The Brexit vote was a case in point. Despite what others may think and say the Leave result was essentially a protest vote against the Establishment, parliament and politicians by a large section of the population who felt disenfranchised, forgotten and condemned to the scrap heap. Like the Palace of Westminster itself, these venerable institutions were falling to pieces, propped up by its members well-meaning belief that everything would be fine, they would pass a few more laws written on vellum and everybody would be happy. It was a dangerous game to play, rough times might be just around the corner.

His visit to the Department of Education had been interesting. Why were they falling over themselves to support his school and headteacher? What game was Rachel Evans playing? It might be something as simple as she was keeping well-in with the institution with its hands on the purse strings. No, it had to be something more than that. His phone rang. It was Debbie, the office manager back at school.

'Hi Mike, just thought I'd call you while you were down at parliament, I've found something whilst looking for influential and famous alumni.' Debbie always managed to find the odd footballer, public figure or celebrity who might be willing to come back to their old school for prizegiving events, as role-models to the students. 'His name is Tony Edwards and he's an MP in the south of England, he was one of our pupils in the early nineties. You might be able to look him up.' He thanked her, wrote the details on a piece of paper and stuck it in his suit pocket.

He sat back in his seat thinking how much things had changed in such a short space of time. There was a time when things looked like they would last indefinitely, a time when there was a clear line in the sand between them and us, when everyone knew which side of the fence they were on. Was Brexit the first crack in the wall of the latest order? Has the whole European project been built without solid foundations and would it eventually crumble away like other continental dynasties and empires? Napoleon's empire lasted around fifteen years, the apparently invincible Third Reich even less. Another empire that had its border in the heart of the European Union's most enthusiastic capital city looked like it would hold onto power with an iron fist, forever. He had seen it up close and would never have believed it could fall...

Chapter 6
1985

Mike had been flicking through one of the many art journals and magazines that came through to his department, it was Easter 1985. These were useful for lesson planning as many of them focussed on an individual artist or movement in art. The magazine cover had first attracted him, a strange mish-mash of old monochrome magazine photos of young women collaged together and set in a background of blues and dusky pinks. It was called 'Da-Dandy' by Hannah Hoch. It was a genre that had flourished during the Weimar Republic in Germany and grew out of Dada, that odd form of expressionism that appeared to throw away all previous concepts of western art and became known as 'anti-art.' He recognised the style at once. At college one of his tutors, an old-time Marxist with a Trotsky beard to match had spoken for hours on end about German expressionist art during the 1920s and the decadence of the Weimar Republic being partly responsible for the rise of the Nazis. Mike had found the politics somewhat boorish, but the art fascinating. He popped the journal into his briefcase to read at home.

He was almost 28 years of age and feeling down with life. He felt he had come to a sort of crossroads which had no doubt been brought on following the death of his father a few months earlier. Mike had sat at his father's bedside in hospital as he was slipping away from life. He had cancer of the pancreas and although sedated spoke with surprising lucidity. He had told him that he was proud of his only child's achievements and that he needed to look after his mother after he had gone. Mike had held his hand as he had gone on to say that he hoped he would give her grandchildren. A few minutes later he died.

His mother had taken everything well but as Mike looked at her as they finished dinner he could see clearly that she had aged. She had begun to clear the table and asked him if he would be going away this summer, going on to say that she thought it would do him good. He told her that he hadn't made any plans and anyway, didn't want to leave her by herself. She came in from the kitchen and sat down at the table next to him.

'Michael, your father and I always wanted the best for you. You work hard and deserve a holiday each year. When you've been away in the past you've always come back like a new man. We never had the opportunity to travel abroad when we were young, or the money, you have, make the most of it son.'

'But what about...?'

She anticipated what was coming and waved her hand in front of her. 'Now don't worry about me, I know that's what's wrong with you. I'm fine, I have my friends, my church club, and your Aunt Teresa from Ireland has said she will pop over and see me this summer.'

'Are you sure?'

'Yes, I am'

'OK, if you're going to be fine. I hadn't thought about it for this year, but thanks anyway Mum'

After dinner, he nipped out to the local shop for some milk. He walked through a chilly drizzle along dark, uninviting streets. He pulled up the collar on his coat whilst thinking about his mother. Would she be alright by herself? He could do with some sunshine somewhere; his own city was bleak and uninspiring. He walked down the side of Anfield and reflected that the football was just about the only thing left working in Liverpool. At least both clubs were doing well these days, a small spark of hope in a devastated city. He bought the milk and went outside. Heavier rain and colder too. He was thinking about last year in Serbia, Bosnia and Croatia, sunshine in more ways than one. He was itching to get away somewhere, but where? Was he getting a little old for back-packing around Europe? His travels had changed him, surely for the better. It had made him explore other societies, see what else was on offer in Western and, to a lesser extent, Eastern Europe. It had also developed him politically, not in the insular homegrown sense but in the wider, cosmopolitan arena. During the past six years he had visited France, the Low Countries, Ireland, Denmark, Sweden, Spain, Italy, Greece, Austria and Yugoslavia. He felt a strong affinity with the people and cultures of Europe and could see clearly the impact of European culture on his own city and country. The world was a big place. He hadn't been to America, Asia or Australia or most of the countries of Eastern Europe including the Soviet Union. There was somewhere else he needed to visit on the continent, he would need to give some thought to that first.

He shouted to his mother as he came through the front door, shook off his coat and took the milk through to the kitchen. She made him a cup of tea and he took it through to the front room, made himself comfortable and opened his briefcase.

Photomontage in Berlin
A new exhibition in Berlin sheds light on art used for political propaganda, satire and publicity.

A small private gallery in West Berlin will host a collection of Photomontage works from the 1920s with several items loaned from the communist East in what could turn out to be a landmark exhibition. We talk to the curator about her long campaign to use art to thaw East/West relations.

He read through the feature and made a written note of the curator's name and the address of the gallery in Kreuzberg, presumably an area of Berlin. He went to a bookcase and rummaged for a book called *Photomontage* before sitting down again. An hour later his mother knocked to check if he wanted anything. He put the book down and asked her to sit down. She sat on an upright chair rather stiffly; this had been his father's room before he had inherited it last November. She felt that she was somewhat an outsider when she was there.

'Mum, provided you are happy, I will go away in the summer, but I promise I will keep in touch.'

'That's fine Mike, don't worry about me, where are you off to this time?'

'Not sure yet, maybe Germany... Need to make a few enquiries first.'

He looked at her face, she looked unsure.

'Are you ok with that Mum?'

She hesitated before saying quietly, 'Germany... Your father wouldn't be very happy, you know with the war and so on, he was on the docks then, lost some of his mates with the bombing. Aren't there still problems in that country with the Wall and things?'

'Mum, the war was a long time ago and I would be going to the West, the problems are in the East.'

'I'm sorry son, you go where you want, you need a break. Enjoy yourself.' She cheered up and smiled. 'I remember the boys coming back home in the fifties after doing their National Service over there, they used to say the German girls were so pretty. We thought they were just trying to make us jealous, which I'm sure they were.' She smiled and even laughed at the recollection, got to her feet, walked over to him and stroked his hair. 'Anyway, we're all in Europe together now, so they tell us.'

The next day on his way home from work he called into the Students' Union travel agents close to the university. The woman behind the counter recognised him as one of her regulars. He asked her for any information about travel to and accommodation in Berlin. She gave him several brochures and said she would sort out an accommodation list and travel options for him if he called back tomorrow.

That evening he browsed through the brochures. In addition to the Western part of the city he noticed that several of them were about travel to East Berlin. After half an hour, he took a small type-writer from a cupboard and set it up on the table.

Dear Fraulein Müller

I recently read with some interest an article about your gallery and forthcoming exhibition...

The following day he picked up the accommodation list and travel details to Berlin from the shop and that evening set about planning his next trip to Europe.

The café was across the road from the small pension he was staying at in Kreuzberg. He had chosen the hotel because it was about half a mile from the gallery and was cheap. In fact, most things seemed cheap here which was surprising as the locals appeared to enjoy an excellent standard of living compared to the economic and social problems besetting his own country. Although he had only arrived two days ago, he observed a vibrant city, spacious, bright, leafy and most surprisingly of all, a friendly city. There were some odd things going on as well. He had spent the first day just wandering around and noticed how empty the city was of people and especially men. The place seemed new and artificial in some way. There weren't many old buildings, no doubt a result of the bombing and destruction of the war years. He went looking for the Wall and found it as he emerged from a large park near the Brandenburg Gate.

There wasn't much to see here, a few German policemen were wandering about, the odd older person walking dogs. He could just make out the top of the gate from the edge of the park with the large East German flag flying on high. He stayed close to the tree line and stood and looked at this side of the Wall from about 20 metres away. It was certainly higher than he had expected, around 12 to 14 feet and constructed of grey, interlocked concrete slabs. He made his way due south across the road from the wall. A few vehicles passed but the whole area was generally quiet and depopulated. The Wall began to bend inwards towards the west making the road narrower as the traffic increased. Then he saw a green open-topped military Land Rover coming towards him with four British soldiers on board wearing their familiar berets. A small Union flag fluttered from an aerial at the back and as it passed he saw the soldier in the front passenger seat holding a submachine gun across his chest. He stopped and pondered that this army patrol represented a continuity going back to 1945. Perhaps for the last 40 years, at this time of day, four British soldiers had patrolled this place, a legacy of the most terrible conflict in the history of mankind.

He continued along to a more open area with some apartment buildings and cafés dotted about. A bus drove by as the parkland gave way to a built-up area. The height of the Wall made it impossible to see the other side unless you were well back or up high. He paused at a bus stop and looked about. A few yards away a kiosk sold drinks, ice-cream and postcards. He drifted over and saw that the postcards showed pictures of the Wall which he thought a little strange. In another time and place this area may have been a tourist spot with the pretty park and ice cream kiosks except there was one problem; the unsightly, grey monstrosity that split a city in two.

There were more people around now but not the crowds that one might expect to see in London or Paris. Everyone just seemed to be going about their business, women with prams, young men and girls on bikes and a group of young children walking together, all seemingly oblivious of a grey concrete wall a few metres away. He looked up at the sign at the bus stop in black gothic letters, it read Potsdamer Platz.

He continued south for a short distance where the Wall suddenly did a sharp left turn towards the East. Before he crossed the road, he passed a large sign that declared 'You Are Now Leaving the British Sector' this was matched by another on the other side which stated, 'You Are Now Entering the American Sector'. As if to confirm this two jeeps drove past him with American troops wearing white helmets and bristling with guns. They turned sharp left and drove off southwards. This was a unique and surreal city, unlike anywhere he had been before, probably unlike anywhere else in the world.

Mike finished his breakfast, the waitress cleared the table and brought him coffee with several newspapers, mostly in German but also the *Washington Post*. His own hotel did not serve meals and the woman manning the small reception area had suggested the café across the road. Everything appeared incredibly laid-back, structured, easy-going, English speaking and liberal. Perhaps he had a far too stereotyped picture of Germany and the Germans before he arrived, one left over from 1945, of militarism, concentration camps, U-boats and the Gestapo, or just maybe that was then and this was now.

He looked through the *Washington Post*. President Reagan was lobbying Congress for more spending on defence. America appeared at ease with itself, prosperous, powerful and pervasive. In Berlin that was certainly the case, their troops and military police seemed everywhere in this area and there was an airport nearby, several large military transport planes had flown in as he looked out from his hotel window this morning.

He put the paper down, finished his coffee and took out his small red *Baedeker* guide and map to find a route to the Gallery Müller. The waitress was saying *'Auf Wiedersehen'* to a couple of customers as they left and held the door open for them. She cleared their table and began brushing the café floor. Mike opened the map of the city out on the table, found Kreuzberg and the street with his hotel that he had previously marked with an 'X' in pencil. A green line ran from north to south down the map with a salient pushing into the west in the centre. The Wall. He looked up and watched the waitress, still tidying up and brushing the floor. She gave him a pleasant smile and he decided the map could wait, he would much rather watch her.

He walked to Gallery Müller later that morning. It was tagged onto the end of a new apartment block but was one of the few remaining older buildings in the area. It probably had been the surviving end of a block of apartments that had been obliterated by British or American bombs or Russian shells. It had a sandstone front with old fashioned stone steps up to a closed front door. He looked at the brass plate and its gothic letters, 'Galerie Müller'. He rang the doorbell and while he waited for a response looked at the sandstone. From ground level, upwards for about three metres there were thousands of small indentations in the stonework interspersed with some random larger holes. The sandstone looked like it had been sandblasted clean recently and Mike presumed the original architect had built the effect in, perhaps with the knowledge the building would be an art gallery.

An old lady with white hair, small and stooped opened the door. She spoke in German so he handed her the letter Fraulein Müller had sent him and announced himself as Herr McCarthy. She gestured for him to wait and walked off. A few moments later a tall woman came down the hallway and shook his hand.

'Herr McCarthy, I'm so pleased to meet you, I'm Ingrid Müller, please come in, I've been expecting you.' She took him into a small room just off the hallway which was half-office, half-lounge. He took a seat in an easy chair and she remained standing.

'May I offer you some refreshment?' Before he could answer she rang a small bell on her desk.

'This is an honour, Herr McCarthy. When I received your letter, I was so pleased someone from England wanted to visit my gallery.' She was a distinguished looking woman in her early 60s, dark, greying hair and dressed impeccably in a black trouser suit. The old woman returned and Ingrid Müller asked him would he like coffee, tea or orange juice. He asked for tea and Fraulein Müller spoke to the old lady who bowed and left the room.

'You must excuse Paula, Herr McCarthy, she has been with me for almost 50 years but I'm afraid she speaks very little English.'

'It's not a problem and if I may say so, you speak excellent English and please do call me Michael.'

'Ah, you are so kind, I learnt a little before the war and since then it seems that the whole of Berlin speaks English... But enough of me, please tell me a little about yourself... Michael.'

After tea, she showed him the exhibition explaining that she had struggled for years to get the East German government to agree to have some of the works displayed in the west. The collection included exhibits by the German artists Hausmann, Hoch, Heartfield and Max Ernst, as well as a couple of Soviet artists he hadn't heard of. She told him that they had held a grand opening three weeks ago, with representatives of both German governments and the four allied powers present. She went on to say that the British Ambassador was most appreciative, however, she had heard one of the American guests say to one of his colleagues, 'Commie Crap'. He saw her smile as she said this. He smiled back.

Mike had noticed that the inside of the gallery had been extensively rebuilt yet some scorched and blackened beams remained and had been varnished over, contrasting with the stark white-painted walls. He asked her about this.

'This house was my home in Berlin when I was young. In 1943, the Royal Air Force carried out a particularly heavy raid one night which destroyed almost all the buildings in the street. We had sheltered in the nearby underground station and returned the following morning. This house was the only one standing. The windows were smashed but after a few repairs we were able to live here until April 1945.'

'What happened then?' he asked.

'The Russians had surrounded the city. My parents, my sister, Paula the maid and myself waited here for the end to come. As the fighting grew worse SS troops came to the house, threw us out and set up a defensive position. We took shelter in a bombed out building with a few others, until the Russians arrived.'

Mike said nothing for several moments, then, 'but your parents, sister...'

She looked at the floorboards and said quietly, 'No... Paula and I were lucky to survive. Afterwards, when the Americans arrived they took her away to hospital, she was close to death. I found the house again. The roof was gone and the floors had collapsed but the shell and the beams were intact. It stayed that way for 15 years until I managed to persuade the city authorities to restore the building. The beams are part of the original house.'

She looked at him and smiled, 'Enough of the past Michael, you are a young man with most of your life ahead of you, enjoy it while you can, Berlin is not a city for sadness, but for reconciliation and love.'

She took his arm as they walked to the next part of the gallery. Later, as she said goodbye to him at the front door he noticed tears in her eyes. As he walked down the steps he looked back at the building and the unusual markings in the sandstone. He realised they were bullet and shrapnel holes.

He walked back towards the hotel, the weather was now hot and sunny and he wanted to get rid of his jacket. He dropped the jacket off at his room and pocketed the map of Berlin, all he would need to explore this afternoon. Kreuzberg was fine but a little quiet, over towards the big park and the Wall was quieter still; there must be a busy area with lots going on, he would look for somewhere like this today. As he stepped out of the front door of the hotel he looked across at the café, hesitated then crossed the road, a cool drink and maybe...

He was served by a different girl and he asked her if the blonde waitress who was here this morning was available.

'Maria... No, she only works in the mornings, can I leave a message for her?'

'No, its fine, will she be here tomorrow morning?'

'Yes of course,' she said. He nodded his approval.

He took out his map and asked, 'I wonder could you direct me to the centre of the city, you know, where it all happens.'

She smiled, 'Yes, I know what you mean. We have a new city centre these days now we are two cities, let me show you on your map. This area here, right in the centre next to the zoo, this is where you will find most things. Look out for the Memorial Church and the Europa Centre with the Mercedes symbol on the top then you can head to the Kurfürstendamm, just here, with lots of cafes and shops.'

'Thanks, I'm sure I'll find it.'

'*Auf Wiedersehen*, have a good day.'

The following morning, he was up and about early, the day promising to be glorious with an unbroken blue sky and already warm. As he showered and shaved he thought about yesterday up in the city centre. As soon as he had walked out of Zoo Station it was if he had stepped into a different city with crowds of people everywhere, shops, bars and restaurants at every turn. He found the Memorial Church, a blackened stump which was obviously left as a reminder of the horror of war. It was attached to a new glass and concrete building in a striking hexagonal shape. He looked up and saw the Mercedes symbol atop the Europa Centre tower block, before walking down the Kurfürstendamm .

The pavements were wide with every few metres glass boxes displaying items from adjacent shops or advertising concerts, operas and theatre productions. Everything appeared wealthy, prosperous and modern. There were lots of people about and even a few tourists. A group of middle-aged American tourists were huddled around a guide who was pointing back to the church telling them that the whole area had been destroyed by American bombers in 1943. Further down he saw two military jeeps parked up with British soldiers in red berets and MP armbands milling about. An officer with a pistol on his belt was speaking with a German police officer while two others stood on a street corner. This was obviously the British Sector but his compatriots were far fewer on the ground than the Americans over in Kreuzberg.

He walked the length of the Kurfürstendamm, which gradually became more residential and suburban. Here and there some of the older buildings remained mainly intact and had been tastefully cleaned up. He walked back towards the city centre, ate dinner at a Greek restaurant before deciding to walk back to his hotel. He headed past Zoo Station and into the western end of the large central park known as the Tiergarten. He could hear animal noises as he walked past the zoo before turning eastwards on to a wide, straight boulevard. He could just make out the tall TV tower in the East about two or three miles distant. Near the Victory Column he stopped for a drink at a kiosk as the last of the light reflected off the gold figure at the top. He crossed the road to the centre island and walked around the brown marble base of the column. The surface was indented with bullet holes and some larger star shapes which he presumed were caused by shrapnel. This was a place honed and defined by war and conflict, yet the people seemed pleasant, courteous and, at times, happy.

A knock on the door brought him back to the present. The cleaner was ready to come in, he asked her to wait a few moments. He put on a tee shirt and jeans, picked up his map and sunglasses before heading across the road for breakfast. Maria greeted him with a warm smile and '*Hallo*' and seemed to have reserved his usual table for him, newspapers in place. She came over, took his order and before she left asked him, 'American?' He smiled and paused for effect, looked her in the eye and said, '*Nein*, Englander.' She smiled and bit her bottom lip in approval before he said cheekily, 'German?' This time the smile was wider, she turned and as she walked away towards the kitchen said in impeccable, faux English, 'I will see to your order now sir.'

The food, as usual was excellent, omelette with fried potatoes. He looked at her as she served the other customers. He guessed she was about 23 years old and five feet six inches tall. She was slim with shoulder-length blonde hair and deep blue eyes. She wore a pink tee shirt with a short denim skirt and had the sort of natural tan that many Germans seem born with. She was efficiency itself, taking orders, serving, cleaning up and taking payments all with an outgoing pleasant manner. He wondered how to make the first move, it was a difficult call. She was certainly friendly, but seemed so with everyone else. He knew her name, Maria, so maybe he could work something around that.

She brought him his coffee and he moved the map on the table for her. As she turned away he said, 'Maria, can you help?' The appeal brought an instant response, as he expected.

'Of course, what is it?'

'I'm wondering where to go today in Berlin, can you suggest anything?'

'Have you been to the Kurfürstendamm area?' He was nodding as she said it so she said, 'Would you like to see the Olympic Stadium?' He hesitated, what did she mean?

'Err, yes, that sounds interesting.' He was floundering, she had snatched the initiative away from him.

'I can go with you if you wish, I'm free this afternoon.'

For a few seconds, he was speechless, she awaited his reply.

'Yeah, that would be fine… Great.' She gave the wide smile again, 'Good, we can meet here at 2 pm, will that be ok for you? You're name?'

'It's Mike, and 2 pm will be fine, see you here.'

He checked his watch, he had three hours to kill. He wandered towards the Tiergarten thinking about what had just happened. Maria was clearly younger than him yet had taken the lead. While he was wondering how to handle the tricky task of the first move she had completely outflanked him with a surprise attack. He sat on a bench, shook his head and smiled. There was a sense of confidence and efficiency mixed with an old-fashioned, mid-European courtesy about these people; perhaps it used to be mistaken for arrogance. As he was growing up in England during the 1960s there was a deep fear, even hatred of the Germans by many people, especially the working class. Later, he had begun to wonder how a nation that fostered Beethoven, Brahms, Goethe and Schiller could have been responsible for such appalling crimes. Surely crimes are committed by individuals? Nations are not responsible en masse, after all, not everyone was a Nazi. The terrible destruction that had befallen cities like Berlin, Hamburg and Dresden was necessary to cut out an evil cancer let loose on humanity. Perhaps the Wall was simply an extension of that, a kind of ongoing medication to make sure the disease did not come back. Had the people changed? Impossible to tell, after all, he had only been here three days in this island city, this unique, utopian experiment. What he had seen so far was optimistic, perhaps the medicine was working but walls always have two sides, he had seen only one.

As he walked through the café door Maria was leaning on the counter talking to the other waitress from yesterday, she came to him and they left. She had changed into fashionable blue denim jeans, a white blouse with the sleeves rolled up high and white training shoes. They headed for the local underground station where he bought tickets for the Olympic Stadium.

As they sat on a bench in a virtually empty stadium Mike was thinking how incredibly confident and outgoing Maria was. She was in fact only 21, yet her English was flawless, with hardly any noticeable accent. On the train and the walk to the stadium she had spoken constantly about the history of Berlin, her life and politics, especially politics. She was a student at the Free University, studying philosophy and worked in the café part-time during term time and full-time during the holidays. She made it perfectly clear that she didn't agree with the current political set-up in West Germany or for that matter, East Germany, describing the regime there as a bunch of terrorists. Neither was she effusive about the Allied Powers controlling West Berlin, saying it was time, after 40 years, for them to go home. He pointed out to her that the Americans had saved the city and its people during the Airlift. She conceded this point, yet argued that they did it for their own ends – to show the Soviet Union how militarily and logistically powerful they were.

They walked around the huge empty stadium together. He was fascinated by the clean lines of the neo-classical architecture and at college had watched Leni Riefenstahl's film of the 1936 Olympic Games which, at least from an artistic perspective, he considered a masterpiece. He asked her if she had seen it and was surprised by her answer.

'Leni Riefenstahl is a Nazi whore. Despite attempts to decriminalise herself she was one of them. Whatever I might think of her work we must never forget that she worked for Goebbels who was no doubt her lover and Hitler who doted on her like the idiot he was.'

There was no hate, no aggression just a shrug as she said it, with her lovely smile afterwards. She took his arm and said, 'Come on Mike, let's get a drink.' In the splendid café inside the stadium he told her about himself and she listened attentively. She asked lots of questions, about his family, about Liverpool, about Britain and about himself including why he had never married. He had shrugged, laughed and said, 'I really don't know.'

They jumped the train back to the Zoo area and Mike said he thought it was strange that a zoo was right in the centre of the city. She explained that originally it would have been in the wealthy, suburban west of the city while most of the population in the centre, north and east would have travelled to the west for a day out at the zoo. Much of the central area was destroyed during the war so in the western sector a new city centre arose around the Zoo and the Kurfürstendamm. Since 1961 this area had become the centre of West Berlin.

He paused before asking, '1961, when the wall was built?'

She simply said, 'Yes of course' without any emotion. She smiled and said, 'I will show you the Wall Mike and everything it represents, but not now, now we are enjoying ourselves.'

As evening began to fall they walked around the Europa Centre, had a look inside the modern part of the Memorial Church and walked down the Kurfürstendamm looking at the shops and cafes. It was still hot and there were lots of young people sitting outside the cafes drinking and socialising. She linked his arm and he manoeuvred her closer to him whereupon she leaned her head into his shoulder. He wanted to kiss her but decided that it could wait till later and besides, he was hungry. They ate at a German restaurant on Kant Strasse, all the time they chatted about their lives and how their different cultures had shaped them.

Maria Schenk was a native of West Berlin. Born in 1964, her parents and older brother, Karl-Heinz, then five years old, had absconded from the Soviet Sector of the city to the Western Sector in June 1961. Although they suspected something might be in the air, their motive for leaving was to obtain an operation for her father who had a piece of shrapnel embedded in his chest since 1944 when he had been wounded in Italy. There was a long waiting list in East Berlin made longer in his case because he was a former member of Hermann Göring's elite paratroopers. Although never a Nazi, Karl Schenk always refused to join the Communist Party in his factory, another factor that made the waiting list longer. Maria's mother, Anna had packed a small haversack with a few toys for Karl-Heinz, took a small bag with a few toiletries and a change of underwear for herself and her son before walking towards the American Sector. A few yards from the boundary they were stopped by two East German border guards who checked their papers, searched their bags and asked the reason why she was walking into the American zone. She told them that she was going to her sister's house for a few days to support her as she was about to have a baby. They waved her through. At that time, the guards were on the lookout for refugees with heavy luggage, a sure sign they were trying to leave the Soviet Sector for good. Anna Schenk had left everything else behind in their small flat near Alexanderplatz.

At the same time, Karl Schenk boarded a bus in the East that travelled each day to West Berlin. He was not a well man and looked older than his 42 years. To complete the deception, he had taken a small stomach potion available from any pharmacy that made his skin turn quite yellow, an old army trick that he and comrades had once used to get out of training exercises. The vehicle was stopped 50 metres from the British Sector by the guards who boarded the bus. They looked down the bus at the passengers, one walking to the rear where Karl was sat. He must have looked almost 60, the young guard looked at him with some contempt and went back along the bus. They did however, pull a young man from his seat near the front and held him at gunpoint against a wall as the bus pulled away into the British Sector. Karl knew they were looking for the young, fit ones who had no intention of returning to the East. Two months later the Wall was erected.

They had lived for a year with their relatives before the city authorities rehoused them in one of the new apartment blocks in Kreuzberg. Anna was a secretary and got work with the Americans. Karl had his operation but the long-term prognosis was not good as most of one lung had to be removed. He had died in 1970. Karl-Heinz was a successful lawyer with a large practise off the Kurfürstendamm and Maria lived with her mother in the same apartment they had moved to in 1962.

They headed back towards Kreuzberg and Maria said she wanted to take him dancing at one of her favourite bars. He was a bit reluctant but wanted to be with her so gave in and agreed. The bar was in a cellar not far from his hotel and was full of young people which made him feel on the old side, at 27. It was certainly vibrant with everyone dancing and enjoying themselves. Maria spotted some friends, grabbed his hand and headed towards them introducing him to them in a mixture of German and English. He leaned on the bar and watched her dancing with one of the girls from the group. The record playing was 'You Spin Me Round (Like a Record)' as both girls gyrated happily to the music, arms above their heads. She came back to him perspiring with exertion. Mike kissed her gently on the cheek, she looked delighted.

'I know him, the singer of that song, his name's Pete.' he said.

'What, how come? I love that record.'

'He's from Liverpool, used to work in a record shop.'

Roxy Music's 'Avalon' began to play. Maria stroked his cheek, smiled and said, 'Dance with me.'

She put her arms around his neck and pulled their bodies together, Bryan Ferry's sensuous vocals melted any lingering doubts and she kissed him deeply on the mouth, her tongue flicking between his lips.

Chapter 7

He had walked her home and after a long kiss they had agreed to meet again tomorrow once she had finished at the café. She looked up at the sky and into his eyes.

'Would you like to go on a picnic tomorrow?'

He laughed, 'A picnic, I haven't been on a picnic since I was a child... Yes, a picnic would be nice, but where?'

She gave that delighted, childlike look and said, 'Berliners love picnics Mike, let it be a surprise.'

At 2 pm the following day he headed for her mother's apartment. At breakfast, she had asked him to meet her there because she would need some help with the picnic things. She opened the door beaming and he stepped into the hallway where she had a basket and a rucksack ready. He put the rucksack on his back and Maria picked up the basket. He gestured along the hallway and said, 'Your mother?'

'She still works a few hours a day for the Americans, she won't be home till four.'

They headed for the local underground station. Maria wore a casual summer, knee-length dress and had put her hair into two Gretchen braids which hung at the side, brushing her shoulders as she walked. He thought she looked older and beautiful and told her so, whereupon she gave that little half-smile, biting her lower lip, something he was becoming very familiar with.

After a few stops the train emerged into the bright sunlight heading out towards the western, rural extremities of the city. Although there were plenty of seats available they had stood close to each other holding onto a chrome rail, chatting quietly, intimately.

A couple of times they exchanged little friendly kisses as he teased her about where they were heading. All she would say was that it was one of her favourite places.

They stopped at the end of the line at a small station in a hamlet that seemed to be deep inside a forest. As they left the station and walked along a well-beaten, sandy track she explained that it was the Havel Lakes area and a popular beauty spot. Maria told him that she used to come here as a child with her parents and brother and later, after her father had died, just the three of them. The place reminded him of childhood outings from Liverpool to Formby and the Wirral, with woods and sandy soil underfoot, except in those places you were only a short stone throw from the sea. They came out of the cool of the trees onto a beach that ran around a lake. It appeared deserted except for a few people on the other side of the lake about 200 metres away. They walked onto the beach and she said they would sit around ten metres from the tree line as she pulled a blanket from the rucksack.

They sat on the blanket together and kissed, this time passionately. He lay back as she stood up, took off her sandals and undid the buttons on her dress letting it drop to the ground. She removed her underwear, crouched down and pushed it under the dress. Leaning across, she pecked his ear gently and said, 'Now you.' As he undressed she stood on the beach, hands on hips looking out at the lake. He looked at her shapely buttocks and back, her long legs and waited for her to come back on the blanket. Maria looked back over her shoulder and said, 'Follow me,' setting off for the lake. They walked together into the clear water up to their waists then turned and held each other. They kissed deeply, her hand dipping down into the water between his legs, searching and stroking. She moved away slightly, took both of his hands in hers and said, 'Come, let's swim first.'

Mike found that any cultural inhibitions he may have held were quickly dispelled. They had swum for 15 minutes, occasionally laughing, often kissing, dried off and made love on the beach. Wrapped in towels they ate their food, drank bottles of orange juice and simply looked at one another, smiling. Some other picnickers came onto the beach, waved and gave a cheery '*Hallo*.' Maria told him that during the summer people came after work, staying well into the evening, meeting friends, eating and drinking. He noticed that naked bathing appeared to be the norm amongst the new arrivals and speculated how the group would have reacted if they had arrived an hour ago, when they were both sexually entwined. He asked Maria who just shrugged and said, 'The same as they reacted when they saw us eating.'

The journey back was all about a deep closeness between them. Exhausted, this time they sat together on the train her head tucked into his shoulder. At the lake, she had asked him how long he was planning to stay in Berlin. He had told her that he had initially booked his hotel for two weeks but had checked with the concierge and he could extend the time if he wished as the hotel was under-booked. He had already made up his mind that he would stay longer. Before they reached Kreuzberg she asked him would he like to go to a political meeting at the university tomorrow night. He told her he would be delighted.

The following evening, they caught the underground out to Dahlem and the Free University. Maria was back in her jeans and tee shirt, hair down, looking every inch a student. She had told him that the guest speaker was the politician and environmentalist, Petra Kelly, a cult hero amongst the students. As they walked through quiet leafy lanes to the campus she waved to other students she knew. Mike felt a little out of place in his chinos and old work shirt, sleeves rolled up, and Maria sensing this put her arm around his waist and pulled him playfully towards her.

They reached a large open square in front of the main building, modern and spacious like most others in the city. There were dozens of people milling about, by their appearance most of them were students but a few older ones who may have been tutors, one who was giving an interview to a TV crew. Two girls wearing Palestinian scarves and carrying newspapers came up to them. Maria kissed them both on the cheek, took one of the papers and said, 'Stay here Mike, back soon... Speak English for him.' The girls said hello and they chatted in English with him, giving him a paper. He looked across the square and saw Maria throwing her arms around a man about his own age and kissing him tenderly on the cheek. A tutor, a lover, both? She was certainly very friendly with him. The girls wandered away giving their papers to others. He looked over again and saw that she was bringing the man over to him.

'Hello, I'm Karl-Heinz, the brother of Maria.'

Mike gave an inwards sigh of relief as they shook hands.

Karl-Heinz Schenk was 29 years old, dark haired, tanned with high cheekbones and the same charming smile as his sister. He wasn't the usual six-foot-plus alpha-male German but around the same height and build as Mike. He had a lawyer's natural self-confidence and spoke English as well as his sister, albeit with a slight accent. He was dressed in a blue-stripped open-neck shirt, grey trousers and burgundy loafers. As he chatted with Mike Maria looked first at Karl-Heinz admiringly and then towards Mike, looking for approval, which she found as both men chatted away, amicably. They walked off together to the entrance of the main university building where Karl-Heinz told them that he was to meet Petra Kelly but would meet them afterwards in the foyer. Mike and Maria headed into the large theatre and took their seats.

Maria explained that Karl-Heinz was one of Petra Kelly's 'important people' in West Berlin and had negotiated with the DDR to arrange her meeting with their leader, Erich Honecker. Mike wasn't sure exactly what Kelly's politics were, he knew she was an environmentalist, a 'Green', but little else. Maria explained that she was also a great campaigner for peace and disarmament and a united Germany. Apparently, Kelly was a strong believer in uniting the communist East with the West under the flag of the European Union. Mike asked Maria if she and her fellow students felt the same way and her reply was interesting to the say the least.

'Of course, we do Mike. We see ourselves as Europeans. Only as Europeans can we bring a lasting peace to our continent. Do you know Mike, I honestly think you feel the same way, you may not be aware of it but I'm sure you do, I can tell these things?'

Before he could reply a group of people came out onto the stage and the audience started clapping. He could make out Karl-Heinz ushering people to their seats on the stage. Karl-Heinz gestured for a girl to head towards the lectern and had with him at the side of the stage a small short-haired lady who Mike presumed was Petra Kelly. The girl began to speak in German and Mike realised she was one of the two girls with the newspapers, who had spoken to him earlier. The girl was obviously giving an introductory speech because every now and then she would turn and look at the guest until she finished off with a flurry and announced, 'Petra Kelly'.

Everyone in the auditorium rose to their feet in applause, Mike included. Occasionally, during the speech Maria would whisper a short translation of some of the important points. At one stage the audience rose to its feet again, clapping and cheering. Maria was quick to translate. 'She just said that all of Germany should be demilitarised, the Americans, British, French and the Russians should take their troops home and let us build a strong, peaceful, prosperous Europe, together with our brothers and sisters in the East.'

Afterwards, they met Karl-Heinz who took them to a room where a reception was being held. Maria had spotted someone else she knew and headed towards them and her brother introduced Mike to Petra Kelly.

'Ah, Mr McCarthy, I understand you are a visitor from England,' said Kelly with a soft American accent.

'Yes, that's right, from Liverpool.'

'A city with many problems, I believe?'

'Well, we try our best to overcome things... I understand that you would like to see Germany reunified and are a supporter of the European Union.'

She paused, looking him in the eye and said firmly, 'I think that you may have been misinformed. Germany cannot be united whilst a vicious, criminal regime exists in the East and as for the European Union, it is currently brimming with bureaucrats and bankers who only want to line their own pockets at the expense of the poorer countries of the continent and the world. They would be better employed redistributing those obscene food mountains to the poor in Africa and spending some money on places in Europe that need it most. Your own city would be a case in point. The institution has to change before it would have my backing, although the basic concept is good, if misguided.'

He felt totally out of his depth and was rescued by an older, distinguished-looking man who came over to her before walking her away to meet other people in the room.

Maria found him again and asked him what he thought of Petra Kelly.

'She's certainly a strong woman and I suspect, very intelligent.'

'You're a good judge of character Mike, that just about sums her up.'

The visitors were leaving and Karl-Heinz was showing them out towards the entrance.

Maria and Mike helped themselves to orange juice and Maria asked him what his plans were for tomorrow.

He leaned towards her ear saying quietly, 'To make love with you, all afternoon.'

She smiled her special smile and replied, 'Its Saturday tomorrow, I don't work at the weekends, why wait till the afternoon?'

He was about to reply when Karl-Heinz returned looking delighted at how the event had gone.

'Now you two, let me take you to dinner.'

He was waving away their protests saying, 'I don't get to see my sister enough Michael and you are a guest in our city, so I insist.'

They travelled in his BMW to the Kurfürstendamm where he parked outside a plush-looking hotel, passing the car keys to the doorman who he was obviously on good terms with. They were shown into the smart restaurant and seated by the maître-de, who, like the doorman, appeared to know Karl-Heinz well. Maria and Karl-Heinz shared a bottle of Mosel whilst Mike indulged himself with some expensive sparkling water. The conversation was dominated by politics yet Karl-Heinz was keen to know all about Liverpool, he had only been to London once and wanted to know about the problems Britain was currently facing. Both he and Maria were keen to know what Mike thought of Berlin. He told them that he had only been in the city for a week and as it was his first visit to Germany he was hardly able to give a balanced view. One area he was impressed by was the fact that West Berlin had rebuilt itself since the war. The conversation steered towards the East and Karl-Heinz said that the GDRs reconstruction programme had lagged behind the West. He explained that there were many reasons for this which included the huge amount of resources put into building and reinforcing the Wall, the sluggish and backward East German economy and the overall influence of the Soviets who simply wanted a weak vassal state that they could manipulate and control. Maria chipped in with the fact that the GDR put a vast amount of resources into spying and surveillance and stated that it was 'no wonder our East German brothers and sisters are suffering.' She also added that neither East nor West Germany would ever rise to its full potential whilst it was occupied by foreign powers for their own military and economic ends. Karl-Heinz smiled and said to Maria the situation was far more complicated than that.

After dinner Karl-Heinz offered to drive them back to Kreuzberg but Maria declined saying they would jump on the underground. As they parted Karl-Heinz said they must get together again soon, Maria hugged and kissed him promising to call. They headed back to Kreuzberg in stifling humidity and as they came out of the underground station she said, 'You haven't given me an answer.'

'Sorry, what was the question?'

'Why should we wait till Saturday afternoon before we make love?'

He smiled, kissing her playfully on the lips, 'I'll answer that question with a question... Why not start in about ten minutes in my hotel room?'

The following morning, he was awoken by heavy rain with a rumble of thunder. The night before he had been concerned about getting Maria past the duty concierge but she told him not to worry, the American servicemen took local girls there all the time and anyway she knew the women who worked at the hotel. Later, he had asked her to spend the night with him but she said that she needed to go home as she had to help her mother with the household chores the next morning. This had suddenly reminded him that he needed to contact his own mother as he had been in Berlin almost a week. He had walked her home and they arranged to meet for lunch tomorrow.

After breakfast at the café he went to a nearby post office that had telephone booths available for public use to ring home. Everything was good with his mother who had taken the opportunity during his absence to visit friends on the Wirral and was expecting her sister-in-law to arrive on Monday from Ireland. She had asked him how long he would be away and he confirmed that it would be another week at least, perhaps more. She seemed fine with this, even encouraging which was a relief for him. He headed to the counter to pay the phone bill and picked up some postcards from a display. He felt a little guilty after the conversation with his mother. He had no intention of returning home in another week, the attraction of Berlin being obvious; but there was something more than Maria holding him here. It was tied up with a feeling of being right on the edge of everything that was crucial in Europe and the world. There was something very special about this place that was getting to him, even after one week.

He went to some other booths with pens and paper available to write his postcards. He looked through them picking out a couple to post to his mother. On the wall was a holiday poster for Bavaria with a picture of one of Bavaria's fabulous castles, perched atop a rocky hill. This was the tourist image of Germany that most people in Britain would be familiar with, the pictures on the postcards, much less so. He sent his mother one of the Olympic Stadium and another, a rather drab rooftop vista of Kreuzberg into East Berlin with the TV tower in the distance, the Wall invisible behind buildings. The other two cards showing pictures of the Wall he kept.

It was still raining as he left the post office, his small travel umbrella just about adequate against the downpour. He decided to have a look around the adjacent area. Kreuzberg, whilst not exactly poor, seemed a bit down at heel and appeared to have had an influx of immigrants from Turkey and other parts of Eastern Europe. There were lots of kebab shops, restaurants and vibrant street markets that the immigrants had set up. Many ethnic Germans mixed easily with them around the markets and cafes and the whole area had a friendly, bohemian feel. He popped into a café to escape the rain and ordered a Turkish coffee. The waiter brought him the drink in an ornate copper pot with a long wooden handle and two chunks of Turkish delight on a plate. He thanked the water in German. He was beginning to feel at home in this city. He paid the bill and went to meet Maria.

After lunch Mike and Maria spent the afternoon in his hotel room lying naked in the sultry heat and listening to the rain. There was an old radio in the room and Maria tuned it into a local pop station as it was playing George Michael's 'Careless Whisper'. They lay together for half an hour listening to the music until the opening notes of David Bowie's 'Heroes' started, whereupon Maria held him closer, kissed him gently and began to cry.

'Do you know the story of this song Mike?'

He was kissing away her tears and shaking his head.

She smiled a little, saying, 'David Bowie wrote it when he saw his two friends, an Englishman and a German girl kissing together next to the Wall, it's an anthem to freedom.'

He didn't know what to say, so said nothing.

That evening when the rain had stopped they went for a walk around the local area and ate at a small Turkish restaurant. Over dinner Maria said she expected the weather to be good tomorrow and if so, would take him to see the Wall.

She was right, the following morning was sunny and cooler after the rain. He was up early, even before the American planes flying into Tempelhof. He showered, dressed and went out for a walk. The café was closed on Sundays so he went into one of the many Turkish establishments near to a leafy square. He had arranged to meet Maria at noon at his hotel so he had some time to himself to wander and think. He went into the square and sat on one of the benches near an empty children's play area. He began to think about this new kind of politics Maria, her brother and much of the student community were forging here in Germany. Was it a youthful reaction to the 40 years of polarisation of Europe? Was it a fad or something solid that would last and what was this emphasis on being European? She spoke of little else, when she wasn't love-making. He smiled to himself at this last thought.

He walked around the square thinking about Bowie's song and Maria's reaction. He wasn't aware of the story behind it till she had told him. Just a couple of weeks earlier Mike had seen Bowie on TV performing it at Wembley as part of 'Live Aid'. It was a passionate performance and made more so after what Maria had told him. It seemed an age since he arrived in this strange, island city which was all but cut off from the rest of the world. Things had happened so fast for him; were all the Germans like these people? Was it the same in Cologne, Munich or Hamburg or perhaps more importantly, in East Berlin, Dresden or Leipzig? A couple walked past him and said '*Guten Tag*'. He responded with his own '*Guten Tag*'. They at least believed he was German, or maybe European.

Maria met him at his hotel and together they headed East along the banks of the Landwehr Canal, the deep closeness of yesterday persisting as she hooked her arm into his. As lovers, they were oblivious to most distractions and even the politics was set aside on what promised to be a beautiful day.

After 20 minutes, they headed up some steps to street level and wandered north-easterly through drab streets lined with post-war apartment blocks with the occasional old sandstone building or chunk of dirty yellow brick wall with the inevitable bullet holes that had been the original building material of much of Berlin's working-class districts. They turned onto a small street and there it was just 80 metres away, slicing off the end of the road. Mike saw the abundance of artwork and graffiti for the first time, purple, red and yellow and the pipe on the top which he said was the same as they have on prisons. Maria had commented without any emotion that the whole of the German Democratic Republic was one huge prison.

They walked alongside the Wall on a paved path that sometimes narrowed down to just a couple of metres between the building line and the concrete barrier, then would suddenly sweep out into open, grassed areas where the nearest building was two or three hundred metres away. A few people were around walking dogs or out for a stroll and everyone seemed indifferent to the Wall. Maria had told him that she was taking him somewhere he could view things from an elevated position, that this was the only way to get an idea of what the wall meant to the people of Berlin.

As they strolled towards the old, geographic centre of the city some of the buildings became taller and they stopped at an old brick built warehouse, several stories tall about 30 metres from the wall. They went into the entrance where Maria spoke to an old caretaker in German. The old man was nodding as he came from his small office and unlocked a heavy door, gesturing them inside before closing the door behind them. They climbed up several floors of concrete stairs before Maria pushed open a door which led onto a flat roof surrounded by a short wall. They walked across the roof to the eastern side of the building.

He was totally unprepared for what he saw before him. Stretching away northwards was a 100-metre-wide empty area that sliced between the two cities. It now became clear to him that there was more than one wall between West and East. Looking down below him was the graffitied concrete slab barrier that he was familiar with but until now had been unable to see over. Immediately eastwards lay a 40-metre sanded area that looked as though it had been carefully raked over. In the centre of this no-mans-land was a double barrier of military style tank-traps, iron girders welded together into a star shape and concreted into the ground, hundreds of them. Maria told him that in some early escape attempts people had used cars and even bulldozers to smash their way through so the border guards, or 'Vopos' as she called them, put in the tank barriers. His artist's eye took in the sheer scale and attention to detail that had gone into the planning and construction. This 'Death-Strip' as Maria called it then extended eastwards for at least another 50 metres with arc lights, another raked sanded area, a service road for the guards before a three-metre-high metal fence and another wall made of brick that backed onto buildings in East

Berlin. In the distance was a concrete watchtower in the middle of the Death-Strip.

Maria went to a small wooden cupboard and took out an old pair of binoculars which she handed to him. Mike focussed them onto some activity in the distance. Two guards appeared from a small bunker that backed onto the Eastern wall and headed off down the service road. The optics were powerful and he could make out the two boys who looked barely 20 years of age with submachine guns slung over their shoulders. They took off their forage caps to soak up the sun and chatted to each other as they strolled along. Maria kept up a running commentary as he watched them telling him that they never patrolled singly to discourage escape attempts, many successful escapes had been by the 'Vopos'. Mike asked her what would happen if one ran to the outer wall to try to get away.

She said, 'The other one would shoot him and if they both ran they would shoot them.'

She pointed to one of the old buildings on Eastern side with a flat roof. Mike refocussed the lenses. Two guards with binoculars and rifles were watching every step the other two made.

One week later.

Mike came up the steps from the Kurfürstendamm underground station and checked his watch. He was early but Karl-Heinz had asked him to come early so they 'could talk a little.' He and Maria had met him in Kreuzberg earlier that week for a drink and he invited them to dinner at his apartment. 'Just a little affair, a few family and friends, nothing too special.' Maria would bring her mother by taxi so Mike had made his own way to the West End that evening. He was looking forward to meeting Frau Schenk yet wasn't sure she knew about Maria and him. These Berliners were so laid back and informal he hadn't thought to ask his lover and anyway, he wasn't particularly bothered. Perhaps some of that informality was rubbing off on him.

He found the apartment block in a quiet side street half way down the Ku-damm, as he had taken to calling it. A brass plate on a heavy mahogany door was etched with a simple, K.H. Schenk. He was shown into a spacious hallway by an old, stooped man wearing a black suit, white shirt and black tie. He clicked his heels as he said to Mike.

'Good evening sir, Herr Schenk is expecting you, please wait here.'

The old man went to an adjacent room and used a telephone, speaking in German.

Mike examined some expensive looking modern paintings in the hallway as he waited.

'Michael, this is such a pleasure, I'm so pleased you could come.' He was shaking his hand and gripping his upper arm at the same time but Mike was looking at his clothes. He was dressed in a dark blue suit, white shirt with a dark tie and looked like he could be waiting to meet the US president. Mike was dressed in a pair of beige slacks with an open neck blue shirt.

'I'm sorry Karl, I didn't know it was formal dress.'

Karl-Heinz beamed and said, 'Don't worry Michael, we can fix that, we Germans can be worse than the English at times with our silly formalities left over from a bygone age. Come, follow me.'

They walked along a corridor and into a large bedroom with mirror wardrobes. Karl-Heinz went off rummaging inside them as Mike took in the décor. There was a whiff of expensive decadence about the place. Huge Rothko-style paintings hung from the alcoves and a double bed with black silk covers dominated the room. Mike half expected to see a pair of women's black stiletto shoes discarded in a corner – Karl must be popular with the ladies with his looks. Karl-Heinz returned with a selection of ties and jackets which he laid out on the bed.

'You look about my size Michael and your colouring is much the same, pick a tie.'

Mike chose a maroon, finely woven knitted tie with a straight end and started to put it on. Karl came up behind him holding a black leather jacket which Mike slid his arms in.

'That's perfect Michael, the fit couldn't be better and you look excellent, very like one of our own West Berlin artists.' Mike looked in the wardrobe mirror at Karl-Heinz, standing to his side with a broad smile on his face.

'Come, let me show you around and we can have a drink before the others arrive.'

Mike settled himself in a comfortable easy chair in a beautifully furnished lounge as Karl poured drinks. They chatted about politics, Berlin, Britain and surprisingly, football. It turned out that Karl was a supporter of the local team, Hertha Berlin and regularly went to home games which the team played at the Olympic Stadium. There was a ring at the door bell and shortly afterwards the old servant brought a man and woman into the room. Karl went forward, bowed and kissed the woman's hand before shaking hands with the man. Mike stood, somewhat bemused by the formal hospitality on show as Karl brought them over to him.

'This is Mr Michael McCarthy from England, Michael, this is my aunt Guida and her husband, Dieter. Mike took the lady's hand and bowed before shaking hands with her husband. They chatted in English for a few moments before Karl excused himself to greet another guest with the servant. It turned out that Guida was Anna Schenk's older sister, Dieter was a big, jolly, Falstaffian character who dispensed with formalities straight away by slapping Mike squarely on the back. Karl-Heinz's servant was giving out drinks as he met his next guest, a dark-suited middle-aged man, ramrod straight with iron grey hair. He was introduced as Doctor Erich von Kramer, a senior partner in Karl's law firm. Karl mingled around insisting that everyone should speak English for Mike's benefit and when his mother and sister arrived, dinner would be served in the dining room.

A few minutes later the servant ushered Maria and her mother into the room and Karl went through his little ritual of kissing the back of the ladies' hands. Mike was enjoying all this Prussian formality and decided to join in the fun as soon as he saw Maria. She was dressed in a black, knee-length cocktail dress, black stockings and high heels, her hair up. Long gold earrings completed her look. He bowed and kissed Frau Schenck's hand before Karl introduced his sister.

'Michael, you have previously met my sister, Maria.'

He took her hand, looked her in the eye and said, 'Fraulein

Schenk, I'm so pleased to see you again, I remember our last meeting with great fondness.' He kissed the back of her hand yet cheekily licked it before raising his head. She blushed and he was delighted.

At dinner, they sat opposite each other, Mike teasing her by trying to catch her eye with longing looks. She responded with her lovely smile, occasionally biting her bottom lip, a gesture he now adored. Anna Schenk spoke excellent English, asking Mike all about his homeland and family. Maria had inherited her mother's tall, handsome looks and it was pleasing for Mike to see them sitting next to each other. Kramer had a slightly patronising, authoritative air about him especially towards Karl-Heinz's servant and the female cook who brought the superb food to the table. Guida was quiet and Dieter, the star of the show drank copious amounts of white and red wine which hardly appeared to affect him, and constantly cracked jokes, sometimes in English, sometimes in German.

Later, as Karl-Heinz was about to say goodbye to his guests he asked Mike would he stay for a coffee. Mike told him he would. As Mike said goodnight to Maria he again took her hand, kissed it and told her he hoped he would see her soon. Both men retired to the lounge, Karl flinging his tie to a chair and heading for the kitchen. Mike looked around the lounge taking in the expensive paintings, mahogany furniture and leather seats. It oozed wealth, sophistication and class yet it was a bachelor's pad. If there was one thing missing it was a woman, or rather the influence of a woman or women.

Karl returned with the servant and cook who carried coffee and cups placing them on a glass table in front of Mike who got to his feet and thanked them both for their wonderful food and service. Karl-Heinz thanked them both and told them to go home adding he would see to the coffee. As Karl poured the coffee he told Mike that his manservant, Jacob was Jewish and had been in hiding in Berlin for most of the war but the Nazis had found him in February 1945 and sent him to Oranienburg concentration camp just outside the city. He never expected to survive but somehow hung on till the Russians arrived in April. Half-dead with starvation and maltreatment he staggered back to the ruins of Berlin only to find that his family had been deported to Auschwitz and his house destroyed in the bombardment. Close to death, he had been found by the cook, Hilde who flagged down a British patrol who took him to hospital. She was an ethnic German who had lost her husband and baby son in the bombing yet she nursed Jacob back to health and they married during the Airlift.

Mike sat quietly as he sipped his coffee. Was there no end to the horror that had befallen this city? Was there anyone who hadn't been affected? Even Karl and Maria's generation were having to live with the guilt along with the latest totalitarian terror, the Wall. Karl-Heinz, perceptively, asked him what he thought of the Wall.

'I don't tend to get shocked by things but when I saw it from above I couldn't believe it, Karl. The sheer size and effort that's gone into the whole thing is incredible. Surely, it's impossible for anyone to escape, even the guards.'

Karl-Heinz was serious as he said. 'It's what you can't see that's more frightening Michael, the surveillance, the betrayals, the prisons, the torture and the fear. These are the things that will lead to the eventual demise of the Wall.'

'You really think that things might change? From what I could see the Wall has been built to last forever.' Mike was shaking his head and looked depressed.

'It's not the concrete, barbed wire and tank barriers that will change, it's the people. Change is in the air over there. Firstly, we have big changes starting to take place in the Soviet Union. They know they can't match the West militarily, their technology is light years behind the United States. Secondly, and most importantly, their economy and those of the East European satellites is in freefall, they really are struggling just to feed their people. Gorbachev and some of the younger men know that they have to change and come to some kind of amicable agreement with the West, otherwise the game is up.'

Mike said, 'Isn't it wishful thinking on the German side, Karl? You want to see a united Berlin and Germany but ask the Americans, French, British and the Russians; perhaps it suits them to have the status quo, which unfortunately means the wall.'

Karl smiled his broad smile, the same as Maria's before saying. 'You sound like my sister Mike, which is perhaps not a bad thing. She is young, radical and anti-American like lots of her young friends. I travel to the East occasionally and meet people connected with the government. Yes, some of them are hard-line, some less so. The hard-liners are worried, they see change in the air in Russia, Hungary and Czechoslovakia. They know they cannot survive without their masters in Moscow. Who do you think pays the GDR for their obscene wall, their spying, security forces, army, tanks and prisons? East Berlin, Dresden, Leipzig, Chemnitz and other cities look like lunar landscapes with black, burnt out buildings, piles of rubble and drab concrete slums. Most people have been pounded into submission by a regime that daily bows to the will of Moscow and the KGB. Yet there are signs of hope, many of the younger generation listen to pop music from the west on their radios, want the latest jeans and shirts that the kids wear in West Berlin and don't care anymore about a socialist utopia. This wall will go Mike, sooner than most people think. Revolution always comes quickly and unexpectedly, but there are always warning signs that go unnoticed by the dominant power. We are seeing some of those signs.'

Mike sat still, taking it all in. Here was someone who had been to the other side and seen for himself the workers' paradise. His lawyer's mind cut through the propaganda of both sides and gave a jurist's verdict. The Wall itself was all but impregnable but if the people on both sides wanted change then who knows? Karl had awakened his curiosity and there was something he had to ask him.

'What's it really like over there Karl? I'm asking because I know I can trust your judgement.'

Karl-Heinz thought about it for a few moments before he said. 'As a lawyer, you are always looking for witnesses. They are worth far more than written testimony and all the flowery language I may speak to a judge. What I'm trying to say Michael is why don't you become your own witness, go over and have a look for yourself. Only by doing this can you formulate your opinion of the East and its place in the world.'

'They would let me, just go through the wall, just like that?'

'Yes, as a foreigner you can enter for 24 hours. You must purchase at least 25 marks of their useless Ost money, they are desperate for foreign currency. You would need to cross at Checkpoint Charlie in the American zone, it's that simple.'

Mike smiled. 'Would you come with me? I'm not sure Maria would be too keen on the idea.'

Karl-Heinz was serious and took a deep breath. 'As a West Berliner, I do not have an automatic right to enter East Berlin, yes, I have been on diplomatic business but I must apply for a visa, several months in advance. It would be the same if I was to accompany you Mike and anyway, no doubt would be refused if I was facilitating someone from what is in effect, an enemy country.' He smiled a little at this.

'You're right about Maria. She hates the whole concept of the Wall and the GDR and would see a visit as a prop to the regime. When she was at school she played volleyball and the school took part in a 'goodwill' sporting tour of East Berlin. I think she was about 16 at the time. Although captain of her team, she refused outright to go to the other side and held a sit-down protest in the road outside her school.' He laughed a little, 'very un-German of her.' He winked and said, 'more of an Anglo-Saxon attitude, I think.'

Mike got the joke and smiled as Karl poured more coffee and opened a box of cigars. 'Can I tempt you with one of these?'

Mike saw the seal and smelt the unmistakable aroma. Cuban. He took one and said, 'Well, tonight has certainly been pleasant for me, let's make it more so.'

Karl lit their cigars with a large marble lighter. Both men inhaled, enjoying the experience and Mike said, 'Don't tell me Karl, they were given to you by a grateful East German Politburo for service rendered.'

He was laughing as he said, 'I'm afraid you've been reading far too much John le Carré, Michael. It's not as sinister as that. Every Sunday afternoon a US air force sergeant from Tempelhof dons his jeans and tee shirt before heading to a flea market in the Tiergarten with a kitbag full of Castro's finest tobacco, no doubt obtained unlawfully from the hold of one of those huge aircraft you see flying in each morning.'

They both grinned and inhaled.

After a short period of silence Karl-Heinz said quietly,

'You know she's in love with you, Mike.' It was a statement, not a question.

'What? Maria... Are you sure?' He was genuinely shocked by the revelation.

Karl was smiling and leaning across from his chair towards Mike.

'It's often the truly lovestruck who don't realise they are in love. Am I sure about Maria? Absolutely.'

'What makes you so certain?'

'She told me, but to be frank, she didn't need to.'

Over the next weeks, Mike and Maria were inseparable. They discussed politics for hours on end and made love every night in his hotel room. They went for another picnic and swim, climbed up the old Radio Tower with lunch in the restaurant and went to see Herbert von Karajan and the Berlin Philharmonic performing Mahler's First Symphony in the Philharmonic Hall.

During the performance, Mike shut his eyes and thought about the past four weeks. He had kept in contact with his mother and told her that he might stay until the end of August. He would need to be back at school at the start of September. The previous evening, he had taken Maria to an expensive restaurant close to the Europa Centre. She wore a short navy-blue dress, high heels and her hair up. He had been teasing her about her dress at Karl-Heinz's and this was her response. She looked stunning and he felt so proud and protective of her. Did this mean he was in love? He wasn't sure, unlike Maria who had told him that she loved him during the meal. She waited for a response but the best he could muster was a lustful, 'I want you', which made him feel cheap and silly. This appeared to affect Maria less than it did him. She smiled seductively and said 'Later.'

The crashing cymbals at the start of the final movement brought him back to reality and as the strings soared into the passionate, romantic main theme, he looked at Maria. She was beautiful, intelligent and desirous. What more could he want? There was little, if any cultural difference between them. They agreed on most things, including politics. They had discussed him staying, or at least returning to Berlin. Maria had told him that there were plenty of jobs available with the British and American forces and housing concessions were available. There was no difficulty between them during these chats. She wasn't pushy or possessive, merely informative. He made up his mind. After the concert, he would tell her that he would stay in Berlin and more importantly, that he loved her. There was now no doubt in his mind about that.

The audience broke into spontaneous applause for the aging conductor and his musicians who von Karajan had taken to the pinnacle of world music. They walked down the steps from the hall arm in arm into the warm night. It was dark, yet ahead of them was the eerie sea of light in no-man's land, silent yet deadly, brilliant but divisive. They headed instinctively towards the light.

They were at Potsdamer Platz, he recognised it from his first look round Berlin. Now ethereally quiet it was hard to believe that it had once been the busiest intersection in Europe. Things change, cities change, politics change. Nothing lasts forever, not even the Wall. They crossed to the East side of the road next to the wall to head back to Kreuzberg and she pulled him towards her saying, 'Remember the song and the story of the two lovers at the wall.'

They kissed until they heard a car horn, looked around and heard a shout in broad Scouse, 'Hey mate, I like yer girl!'

A British Army jeep was driving past slowly, the two squaddies laughing. Maria waved to them and Mike laughed, telling her about the young soldier's accent.

She held him close again saying,

'Does it make you a little bit homesick?'

He kissed her deeply, and whispered into her ear, 'How could I be homesick when I'm with someone I love?'

The following morning, he lay on his bed in the hotel room looking up at the ceiling. Was the attraction of this place just Maria or was it the city itself with its unique idealism, its citizens living, literally, up against a wall? Perhaps the West Berliners' liberal, carefree attitudes came from knowledge they were first in line should the world go mad again. Maria had told him that there were places in the wall specially constructed to allow the Soviet and East German tanks to pour through at short notice. Did all these things conspire to make the people like those of San Francisco who lived with the knowledge that at any time another catastrophic earthquake could destroy them? Here the earthquake would be man-made and therefore, far more destructive.

Since his arrival in the city one thing had been eating away at him: what was it like on the other side? Karl-Heinz had explained how simple it would be to cross over for a day and look. In a round-about way, had encouraged him to do so. Mike had never been one to sit back and accept the official line about anything or anywhere, he always had to go and see for himself. He needed to settle down and wanted to be with Maria, maybe children, but that could wait. He would look for work in Berlin, resign from his job in England and return home for a while to make sure his mother was cared for. Who knows, his mother might even come to live in West Berlin, Maria had said she would come to Liverpool to meet his mother. The attraction for him was the package; Maria and Berlin, it wouldn't work any other way.

They were in the Tiergarten when he told her. She had reacted badly. She lost her temper and he was surprised and shaken by her reaction.

'Michael, it's a concentration camp! My German brothers and sisters are treated like scum by a criminal regime that hates everything that I... and you, stand for. I thought you were a man of principle from a country that valued human rights above everything else. How can you even think of going over there like some American tourist in a baseball hat, camera around his neck, smirking at East Berliners in their pathetic clothes.'

He was shocked, looked at her tearful eyes and said, 'I'm not like that Maria, surely you know me well enough to know that?'

She was crying now and turned away from him, put her head down and covered her face with her hands. He tried to put his arms round her but she pushed him away. He was desolate, never had he felt so helpless as he mumbled something about it not being that important and her feelings were more important to him than a concrete wall.

She turned, threw her arms around him kissing his cheek whilst speaking German and brushing her tears away. Her amazing smile returned.

'I'm fine now Mike and so sorry about this, come on, let's go to your hotel.' They hugged before walking away, arm in arm.

'What did you say to me in German?'

She was laughing and said, 'I called you a fucking bastard but also said I will love you forever.'

'I'm sorry for saying you were like an American tourist. You couldn't be more different. I lost my temper, I'm so sorry, my love. You do need to go over there, to see for yourself what I have told you.' She was sitting naked on his bed, back to the wall drinking a bottle of Pepsi. She put the bottle down and sat stroking her leg. Mike watched her, looking at the tiny blonde hairs on her thighs and thinking how much he loved and desired her. She was telling him what he needed to do to cross to the other side, he didn't interrupt and let her continue.

'My mother said she would like you to come to dinner.'

'Does she know about us?'

Maria smiled and sighed, 'Mike, she is a German *mutter*, they know everything.'

'Well, I like your mother so please tell her I will come to dinner. Will I have to kiss your hand again? I liked that last time.'

She laughed, leaning across to kiss him, saying, 'I'm sure you did.'

Mike sat on the steel and canvas chair, his hands folded on his lap. He looked at the young man sitting at the table in front of him looking down at Mike's passport and the papers he had filled in at the counter outside. He can't have been much older than Maria and had blond hair, cut in a short, military style. After a few minutes, he looked up and said,

'Tell me why you want to visit the German Democratic Republic, Mr McCarthy.'

'Out of interest and curiosity for your country.'

There was no flicker of emotion from the border guard officer who looked down at the papers again. Mike took in the smart green uniform, the fact that he spoke almost perfect English and began to wonder why he found the papers so interesting.

'Where have you been for the past month?'

For some reason, Mike felt his palms sweating and thought carefully before answering.

'Staying in a small hotel in Kreuzberg and looking around West Berlin. I put the address on the forms.'

'Yes, I know. I see you are from the city of Liverpool. An interesting place with lots of fine buildings, good football and of course, the Beatles.' Mike didn't reply despite the officer looking at him. The officer continued speaking.

'Unfortunately, a city with many problems, a city let down and abandoned by your government. Are you, as the English say, a political animal Mr McCarthy?'

Mike paused before replying. What exactly was he getting at? 'I'm a teacher, I don't get involved in politics.'

The officer looked up from his papers, raising his eyebrows slightly. There was a slight trace of a sarcastic smile as he said.

'Really? I see that you have written that you visited Gallery Müller and the photomontage exhibition. These are political artworks, many have been loaned to this gallery by my government as an act of goodwill. As an art teacher, you will know that they were courageous acts of defiance against Fascism. They are just as relevant today as when they were first produced, wouldn't you agree?'

'I appreciate the political message in the works. Many visual art works contain political messages, some obvious, some not so obvious. I'm pleased that your government has made these important works available to a wider audience.'

The East German looked pensive. He collected the papers together and put them into his briefcase. He picked up Mike's passport and handed it to him, stood up and held the door open.

117

'Welcome to the capital of the German Democratic Republic, Mr McCarthy. I can recommend Museum Island, I'm sure you'll find it most interesting.'

The walk to the Unter den Linden passed without him noticing much at all. He was preoccupied by the interrogation, or was it an interview? Maria had told him that he might be questioned about his visit but all the same it had been sobering. He began to piece things together. He began to take in his surroundings in East Berlin. The buildings generally had not been cleaned or renovated as well as those in the West, however, there seemed little difference between the two cities at this point, except there were no commercial advertisements to be seen. The country's flag was flying above most buildings and he presumed he was in a government area.

He turned onto the Unter den Linden, once the pre-war city's most famous street and looked left to see the Brandenburg Gate about 400 metres away. He needed a map and found a small newspaper kiosk in the centre of the boulevard. He was about to speak in English but remembered that Karl-Heinz had said he would need to speak in German as most East Berliners were not strong English speakers. He found a map on the kiosk, pointed to it saying, '*Karte bitte*' to the man behind the counter. He handed him a ten ostmark note and received several notes in change. He decided to walk towards the Brandenburg Gate and noticed the people. The street was quiet and most appeared to be office workers walking from building to building. There were plenty of Vopos around as he approached the Gate and he stopped before he reached a waist-high barrier which marked the furthest he could go. He knew that this was part of the Wall yet it was innocuous compared to the heavy military fortifications he had observed with Maria. On the far side of this famous building, so symbolic of Berlin he could just make out a white-painted wall which must have been the same wall he had seen from the other side on his arrival which now seemed a lifetime ago. He began to retrace his steps and opened his map when he reached a junction.

'*Kann ich dir helfen?*'

He looked up from his map into striking green eyes. A woman

about his own age was looking at him and pointing down at the map.

'Sorry, err, *ich spreche kein Deutsch*, do you happen to speak English?'

'Yes, a little, perhaps I can help, *mit Ihrer Karte*, sorry, bitte, please show me your map and where you will go.'

Mike couldn't think of anything to say except, 'Museum Island.'

She pointed down at the map, drawing a line with her finger along the Unter den Linden then pointing in the direction of the TV tower as she spoke. He looked at her appearance. She wore a tight-fitting, dark-green, knee-length skirt suit, the type that had been fashionable during the 1960s. Pointed shoes with two-inch heels, tanned bare legs and her dark hair worn up gave her a dated, yet attractive look. She could have been in Swinging London, 20 years ago.

'Please don't forget to turn at the Dom, or as you say, the cathedral.'

She gave him a smile and flirtatious look as she wished him a pleasant visit to Berlin.

He watched her as she crossed the road. She was no different from the girls in West Berlin, helpful, pleasant and attractive. The only visible difference was the fashion sense which wasn't important, it's the person beneath that counts.

This whole area was the city centre of old Berlin and to the East German's credit they had made an enormous effort to renovate and clean the damaged neoclassical buildings. It was a difficult task; the devastation here had been tremendous. The cathedral was blackened and blasted with teams of workers carrying wood, sand and concrete into the empty structure. All around were vast, empty spaces where the destruction had been total with modern concrete buildings being erected. As he walked up the steps to the Old Museum he saw the renovation work to the classical columns and entrance area. Painstakingly, the authorities had patched up the bullet and shell holes, yet no amount of sandblasting could remove the black carbonisation caused by the ferocious fires.

He lunched in Alexanderplatz at an outdoor wurst café with

families and children looking surprisingly happy. Some teenagers walked past with clothes and hairstyles little different from their counterparts in Kreuzberg, except without branded names. He wished Maria was with him. He was missing her and he wanted to share this day with her. Whatever the regime may do to its populace, one thing was certain in his mind, the people were no different from those on the other side of the Wall. They suffered just as much, perhaps more so than West Berliners because of that crazy concrete barrier. Karl-Heinz was right, if the people wanted it enough, it would happen. Perhaps then, Europe could unite around a common cause, maybe the European Union would be the catalyst for that to happen.

Maria had said she would meet him on the western side of Checkpoint Charlie at 7:30 pm. After lunch, he had wandered eastwards amongst huge, impersonal concrete tower blocks before turning back towards the city centre. It had been a strange day without her by his side. When he returned home he would put things in place to resign from his job, plan to live and work in Berlin and make sure his mother was cared for. When all those things were done, he had decided on something else. He would ask Maria to marry him.

The light had dipped a little as he walked down Friedrichstrasse. It was getting towards the end of August, towards the end of summer. The evenings were starting to turn a little cooler. Maybe they would have time for one more picnic and swim before the weather changes; he would suggest it to her later over dinner.

He passed through Checkpoint Charlie without any fuss, the Vopos on duty handing him his passport and casually waving him through. Well there it was, East Berlin, the other side of the wall. He felt a little deflated. It wasn't a concentration camp, nor was it the worker's paradise but simply one half of a major European city trying to come to terms with its past. The American soldiers on duty gave him even less attention than the Vopos as he stepped into West Berlin and walked down the street into Kreuzberg. The street was empty as he scanned the pavements looking for her. He saw a white BMW parked, the driver got out and walked towards him. It was Karl-Heinz.

Chapter 8
November 2016

'Mike, are you OK up there? You've been in that shower for ages.' The sound of Jane's voice interrupted his thoughts and he turned the water off quickly. From the shower room, he could see his old faithful leather jacket lying on the bed, a jacket with so many special memories. He had been in the shower far too long, lost in a bygone era, now he had to get ready to meet his friend Pete.

The last time Mike McCarthy had seen Pete Smith was a few days after the Referendum. There was a time when they had seen each other most of the time, but then that was at school and as people went off to work, college, had relationships, children and different lives it was inevitable that they would grow apart. He had stayed in touch with Pete, through good times and bad, whatever the economic or political weather. They were opposites in most respects which was possibly the reason they had remained good friends over the years. Mike zipped up his jeans, pulled on a sweat-shirt and picked up his old black leather jacket, knowing straight away Jane would object. Lately, she had been trying to get him to bequeath it to a local charity shop. He smiled to himself, thinking about its history, something Jane was totally unaware of.

He walked into the kitchen where Jane was peeling vegetables in preparation for dinner, sat down and looked at his wife.

Without looking up from her task she asked,

'What time are you meeting Pete?'

'Not till 8:30, he's got a job on today and it will be a late finish for him.'

He continued to look at Jane. She wore her cream blouse and black skirt having arrived home only 15 minutes earlier. Mike went up behind her, put his hands around her waist and kissed her neck. She reacted favourably for a few seconds before pulling away, turned around, kissed him on the cheek and said, 'Not now Mike, I've got to get dinner ready.' She looked down, smiling and said, 'Not that old jacket again, I'm going to sneak it out of the house when you're least expecting it.'

'Don't you dare.'

He turned at the junction at the end of his road and onto the wide dual carriageway that formed the main inner ring road around the city. He thought about Karl-Heinz. Where was he these days? They had kept in touch with the occasional letter until the mid-1990s when a typed, formal looking envelope arrived for him from Berlin. It was from a Frau Schindler who was Karl's office manager at his lawyer's practise. Frau Schindler informed him that Herr Schenk had sold the practise and had left Berlin to live in Switzerland. She did not have a forwarding address. Mike knew that it wasn't like Karl to down tools and disappear so decided to ring Berlin and speak to Frau Schindler personally. She was typically efficient and formal in her replies to his questions. No, she did not know why Herr Schenk had sold the business and moved to Switzerland. No, as she had already stated, the practice did not have a forwarding address in Switzerland. No, it was not possible to speak to Doctor Kramer, sadly he had passed away, some months ago, Mike then asked her if she had an address for Herr Schenk's younger sister who he had lost touch with. He detected a pause from Frau Schindler before she apologised, saying that she did not know where Fraulein Schenk lived. It was the last he had heard of Karl, or for that matter, Maria. He felt a pang of something as he thought about both, loss and love, maybe.

Mike saw the yellow petrol light on the dashboard blinking and pulled into the next filling station. Whilst he was filling up, a minibus full of men pulled up next to him. He ran into the building to escape the freezing rain and joined the queue to pay. The attendant was telling the woman in front of him that the minibus was full of Poles who went off to work every morning on 'some office block somewhere' then came back every night about this time. He went on to query why they 'hadn't been thrown out by now because we voted for Brexit.' Mike looked at him and decided not to tell him that we were still a member of the EU, that we relied on foreign workers to run much of our economy and services and doubted we had enough people with either the skills or inclination to get up at the crack of dawn, build an office block in appalling weather and return home at 8 pm every night.

He pulled off the filling station concourse and into the traffic flow. His level of annoyance with people who voted to Leave had receded since the summer when he couldn't go to the local supermarket without looking at fellow customers and deciding who voted Leave or Remain simply by their age, appearance and level of conversation. He realised it was a ridiculous way to try and categorise anyone or anything, a rejection of all the intellectual values he held so dear.

He glanced at his watch and noticed raindrops on his jacket sleeve. It reminded him of the last time he had seen Karl-Heinz. He had come to pick him up at his hotel to take him to the station with his luggage. He was taking his bags from his room, saying he couldn't understand Maria, that she was headstrong and selfish, was refusing to speak to him and behaving like a child. He would get to the bottom of things and find out what was wrong with her. Mike patted his shoulder telling him not to worry, that it wasn't his problem and anyway, it didn't matter. Both knew it was a lie.

As Mike was about to close his room door for the last time he suddenly remembered something. He went to the wardrobe and took out Karl's leather jacket. He looked at the bed before locking the door, going downstairs into the lobby and handing Karl his jacket. He laughed, took the garment, told Mike to turn around and put it on him over his t-shirt.

'It's raining out there, you'll need this Michael'

'No, I couldn't Karl, it must be worth a fortune.'

Karl was serious. He put his arms around Mike, hugging him.

'It's not worth anything compared to friendship, my friend.'

He pulled into the pub carpark and sat in the car for a couple of minutes looking at the rain streaming down the windscreen. He hadn't thought about Berlin for a while. From what he could gather the city had changed dramatically since the Wall came down in 1989. He had wanted to visit again but hadn't pushed it too much, even when Jane had suggested they take a break there a few years ago.

Pete was standing at the bar drinking beer and chatting-up the pretty and considerably younger barmaid as Mike walked up behind him.

'Hello big man, I see you still have an eye for the ladies.'

Pete Smith shook his hand saying, 'you know me Mike, I never change, still drinking lemonade?'

'I've moved onto the hard stuff these day, Cola, keeps my dentist in business.'

Pete was laughing as he ordered a Cola for Mike and another beer for himself. The two men sat at a table, completely at ease with each other's company and the friendly small talk, everything from football to the cost of living. Mike told Pete that he was going to be teaching politics from next year and suggested that he would keep a place in his class for Pete. They could both laugh at each other's jokes which were inevitably at the expense of the other. Eventually the talk moved on to the Referendum and Brexit.

'Still a Remainer, Mike, or should I say, Remoaner?'

Mike saw the joke and replied with humour, 'Just because your football team loses a match, you don't stop supporting them.'

'But you're out of the competition Mike. You sound a bit like my wife. She told me last week that she voted Remain. I was completely surprised, didn't even know she'd voted, doesn't normally bother.'

'I've said from day one that I completely accept the result and the fact that we will be leaving the EU. However, it's all about on what terms we leave. We can't just walk-away, the country would collapse economically and socially. We have almost One and half million of our people living and working in the European Union, they have an estimated three million in Britain. What happens to them? Do we order the police to start rounding them up, put them in detention camps and on boats across the Channel? It's just not going to happen is it Pete?'

'I don't know Mike, you were always more into politics than me. What I do know is that I'm a small businessman employing 20 people in my plumbing firm. I struggle to get suitable local lads for the jobs they do. I interview young fellas all the time and they are simply not up to the job. They just don't have the skills that I need, let alone know what a stopcock is. To get the best boys I must employ foreign workers, at least they have the necessary skills. I don't want to do that, but have no choice. I want to see us standing on our own two feet with a highly skilled workforce ready to take the job opportunities currently filled by migrant workers.'

'But that's nothing to do with the EU, Pete. It's the fault of successive British Governments failing to address the very serious social issues that have continued over the decades. Look, we're not a world power anymore and we have only a fraction of the industry we had just thirty or forty years ago, we rely on Europe for our trade and economic wellbeing. Unless we address how we leave, we will have far more serious social issues than we have now.'

'Well, I'm hoping we get a kind of Norway deal, you know, a half-in, half-out situation. That's what we were told before the Referendum, that's what I voted for, I'd be happy with that.'

'I'm not so sure we'll get that Pete. I have a horrible feeling that the whole thing will go pear-shaped, with us walking away with nothing. Some of those countries around Europe will be pissed off at us pulling out for the simple reason that it cocks up their economies and gives some of their extremist groups inspiration to start causing trouble. This whole Brexit thing has started to have a knock-on effect everywhere. Just look at America, every time I turn on the news Donald Trump is saying he's going to win, just like Brexit.'

Pete Smith was laughing now. 'You don't think for one second that he could possibly win do you Mike, come on, credit the Yanks with some intelligence.'

'In a democracy, anyone can win. That's the whole point.'

He drove out of the carpark, not exactly looking forward to the half-hour journey home, the rain relentless. It was always good to see Pete. He wondered why his lifelong friend had voted for Brexit. He was certainly a patriotic type and would much rather employ his fellow countrymen than anyone else, nothing wrong with that sentiment. Mike concluded that Pete probably didn't quite understand all the ramifications of leaving, something he would happily admit to, he was that kind of guy. Mike smiled to himself thinking about Pete's wife telling him she voted Remain. He could just imagine his friend's incredulous face, not upset that she had voted differently, simply astonished that she had voted at all!

He thought about Jane. They had been together for 30 years, a time span that had passed far too quickly. He switched the radio onto a jazz channel and the mellow sounds of Miles Davis infused through the car. Night music supreme. She always loved to listen to cool jazz when they were alone, holding each other. He realised that he didn't know for certain in which box Jane had placed her cross on June 23rd. He presumed she had voted to remain, it was not something they had discussed. Jane was almost completely apolitical, always far more concerned with her family and her young children at school, just as she was the very first time he had met her.

In 1986, Mike was teaching art at his first school, a tough secondary in Liverpool's Dingle area. The area had suffered from the decline of the south docks during the 1970s and was geographically placed next to Toxteth, the part of the city that had become synonymous with the problems that had beset Liverpool during the 1980s. He had come in one morning and found a message in his room from the headteacher asking to see him. Mike put on a tie and headed down to the head's office.

'Thanks for this Mike, I know it's an unusual request but times are changing, perhaps for the better. This primary school is up in Mossley Hill, about four miles away. This eh...' He glanced down at some notes on his desk, 'Mrs Wickham, the headmistress, she's expecting you about ten o'clock this morning. By all accounts she's well thought of down at the local Education Authority, apparently quite progressive, whatever that means.'

Mike jumped in his old VW Polo and headed off into the south of the city. It was an unusual request, apparently, Mrs Wickham wanted to put on an art exhibition in her school of the work of his students. The school was in a pleasant suburban area, well away from all the problems currently besetting the inner city and it was a welcome change to be heading somewhere different on a sunny day in mid-May.

He was shown into the headteacher's office by a secretary. Mrs Wickham turned out to be something of a surprise, younger than expected, mid to late thirties, dressed in a black skirt suit. She shook his hand warmly and gestured him to two easy chairs aside a small coffee table.

'Good to meet you Michael, your head told me that you would be coming this morning.' Scottish, a soft brogue, probably Edinburgh. 'The teacher who will be looking after you has had to cover for an absent colleague for an hour so let me get you a drink and you can tell me all about yourself.' She got up, went to her desk, picked up the phone and ordered coffee from the secretary. Mike noticed how attractive she was. Dark hair piled on top of her head, green eyes, a slim, curvaceous figure with an easy-going manner. He said,' I'm afraid there isn't much to tell you Mrs Wickham.' She came and sat in the chair opposite, crossed her legs and said, 'Firstly Michael, please call me Pauline and now, I understand that you are something of a traveller.'

Mike wiped a tear from his eye. He hadn't laughed this much for years. Pauline Wickham was a very funny and engaging woman. For the past 50-odd minutes, she had regaled him with stories and anecdotes about herself including one a few minutes ago, about a trip to Moscow in her gap year which had brought on a fit of laughter and tears to his eyes.

'Surely, you're kidding me, Pauline. You're telling me that this KGB man at the airport stopped you, took you into an office and said he wanted to strip search you for drugs and you said what?'

'I said, OK Boris, that wasn't his name by the way, I'll get my kit off for you if you get me a pass to the Kremlin and Lenin's tomb.'

'So, what happened?'

'I didn't just get a pass, I got my own KGB guide around the city for the next week, taken to all the best restaurants, art galleries and palaces, free of charge. Turned out he was a pussycat, soft as a brush and despite what you may think, a perfect gentleman. The poor man was heartbroken when I left. That's what they're like, the Russians, the place thrives on corruption, you must do deals with them all the time, just to get through the day.'

Mike was laughing again and shaking his head. He finished his second cup of coffee as Pauline said, 'Right, come on, let's go and see Miss Ashton.' They walked down a corridor where he saw a young blonde woman crouching down with an arm around two young children, one of whom was sobbing. She dabbed away the tears sending both on their way with a smile and stood up. Pauline said, 'Mike, this is Jane Ashton.'

An hour later as Pauline Wickham was seeing him off in the carpark she said, 'Many thanks for your help Mike, Jane will look after the exhibition with you.' She put a piece of paper in his hand saying, 'I'm having a little get together on Saturday afternoon, you are most welcome. Wear your jeans, it's completely informal, out in the garden with food and drinks, it would be smashing to see you again, my address is on there.'

On Saturday morning, he sat in his chair in the small front room trying to decide whether to go to Pauline Wickham's garden party. Was she being friendly or was her invitation a subtle attempt at a pass? She was certainly attractive and great company but he didn't usually start relationships with older women and besides, she was probably married. More to his satisfaction was the fact that he would be taking some paintings to her school next week and he and Jane Ashton would start to put up the art display in the school foyer. He was looking forward to seeing the young teacher again. He glanced down at Pauline's address on the paper and decided to put off his decision until later in the day.

He had lunch with his mother and went up to the spare bedroom. On an easel in the centre of the room was an unfinished painting, a postcard pinned to the top corner of the easel. Mike squeezed paint from a tube onto his palette and started brushing some yellow daubs onto the canvas. It blended in well with the rest of the graffiti on the Berlin Wall. He stepped back, sat on a stool and stared at the picture for 20 minutes then stood up and threw his paintbrush with some venom at the canvas. He wiped his hands with a cloth and headed for the shower. He had decided to go to go to Pauline Wickham's house party after all.

The house was a large, detached Victorian mansion in Sefton Park with several cars parked in the circular driveway. He parked in the roadway outside and walked back towards the house. In the mid-nineteenth century, these houses were amongst the finest in Britain, if not the world. Once the domain of shipping line owners and industrialists they had long since fallen from grace yet still held a certain charm and interest. He heard music and went through a gate at the side towards the back garden. About 30 people were milling around and Pauline headed straight for him, linking his arm.

'I'm so glad you could come Mike, come on let's get you a drink.' She walked him towards a long trestle table and began to pour out some red wine. So, it was looking like a pass after all. He wasn't bothered in the least, she looked great with her hair down, in jeans and a t-shirt. He refused the wine and settled for orange juice.

'You've certainly got the weather for it Pauline.'

'I know, it was a worry but the sun always shines on the righteous, Mike.' She squeezed his arm.

She introduced him to a couple of people before saying, 'Now, there's someone I want you to meet.'

Pauline took him through the partygoers to a rusty old oil-drum with a wire grill on top which was belching smoke. Next to it stood a tall yet corpulent man with a huge apron wrapped around him. She introduced Mike to her husband Bob Wickham who was tossing burgers on the grill.

'I'll leave you with Bob for a few minutes Mike, he'll tell you all about his new toy.'

'Eh... OK Bob, what exactly are you doing?'

'This here is known as a barbeque old-boy. They're all the rage, or so they tell me. Pity about the smoke though, its ruined my rugger shirt. So, you're the young man sorting out the paintings for the school. I'll tell you what, I bet your kids put up a better show than some of these modern art fellas, I can't understand what the hell they're on about with all those squiggles and boxes.'

Bob Wickham was one of life's wonderful characters. He was eccentric, incredibly intelligent and personable. Mike reckoned he was at least 15 years older than Pauline. He had a mop of grey hair, a crimson face and a booming voice that belied an inner gentleness. He was a senior lecturer at Liverpool University's History department and Mike McCarthy instantly took to him.

Pauline returned with a tray and plates. 'Bob, for God's sake give me those sausages and burgers, I'll pop them in the oven, they'll never get cooked on that old thing.' She scooped up the meat and hurried off into the house. Mike wandered around talking to the odd person. Pauline caught up with him again, telling him to help himself to drinks. He went over to the trestle table and started to pour out an orange juice. He felt a gentle hand on his arm followed by, 'Hello.' He looked around to see Jane Ashton.

They were deep in conversation when Pauline found them.

'Hello Jane, so glad you could come, no need to introduce you two, food will be about ten minutes, I must go and rescue Bob from his burner thing, see you later.'

Mike and Jane looked at each other and spontaneously burst out laughing.

They had eaten hot dogs and burgers with salad, discussed the art exhibition and touched on each other's background, likes and dislikes. Pauline had appeared every so often like a mother hen asking if everything was alright. Everything was fine. As the evening wore on he suggested they take a walk in the park. She beamed and nodded.

Pauline headed over when she saw movement.

Mike said, 'We're just going for a walk in the park Pauline, we'll be back later.'

'The park is lovely this time of year, Mike, show Jane the Peter Pan statue. Now, be back for about eight-thirty we're having hot apple pie with brandy.'

After a look at the Palm House and the statues they headed back to the roadway. Instead of turning towards Pauline's house they walked into Lark Lane. A mixture of Amsterdam, Hamburg and Copenhagen it somehow managed to be influenced by those places yet retain its quant, unique Englishness.

'Have you been here before Jane?'

'The first year I arrived I came to one of the concerts in the park with some student friends. Afterwards, we came here for a drink, it's amazing. She laughed, 'In those days I used to get mixed up with Penny Lane, thinking this was the place about the song. I've got it right now, my flat is just off Penny Lane, across the park which is just as lovely, but quieter. I can see where the Beatles got their inspiration from, this whole area is fascinating.'

'It must be difficult for you, such a long way from home.'

'Well, a little at first, but everyone is so friendly and they all seem to have roots everywhere else but end up settling here, like Pauline.'

They walked into a wine bar and ordered drinks before sitting at the bar on stools. Mike said, 'I didn't know you were coming today.' Jane smiled, took a sip of her drink, smiled and replied. 'I didn't know you were coming either, I suspect the hand of Mrs Pauline Wickham in this Mike.' Their hands had momentarily touched on the bar counter and each had left their little fingers entwined. Mike said, 'Perhaps we should go along with her little game.' Jane smiled and blushed a little before they kissed.

Later, they returned to Pauline's to find the last of the guests leaving and Bob clearing up in the garden. Pauline beamed when she saw them, bringing them inside the house before settling them down in the spacious living room. Their hostess returned with plates of hot apple pie, a bottle of brandy and a jug of cream. She poured some brandy into the cream, stirred it and poured it over the slices of pie.

'You make a start on that and I'll help Bob finish off.'

Mike and Jane sat eating on the large settee, occasionally looking and smiling at each other. He wiped a spot of cream away from her lip as Pauline and Bob returned with their own plates, Bob slumped himself into an armchair and Pauline put on some music. An hour later Jane was sitting on the floor at Mike's feet, her head resting on his thigh. Mike looked down at her long, slim body, her natural blonde hair and felt the warmth of her face on his leg. Bob had polished off a bottle of red wine and Pauline was speaking quietly about her childhood in Scotland. Two months later, Mike and Jane visited Paris.

His phone rang, it was Jane, he answered it using the hands-free system in the car.

'I was just thinking of going to bed Mike, how long will you be?'

'I'm about a mile away, wait up for me, I'd like to see you.'

'OK, see you soon.'

Jane Ashton was the best thing that ever happened to Mike McCarthy. She came along at the right time, a time when he had reached rock bottom. She was everything that some others were not; non-political, homely, familial and... English. In Pauline and Bob, they found an older brother and sister, godparents to their children and lifelong friends. In late 1999, Bob had dropped dead at his desk in work. Pauline, devastated, took six months off work to recuperate and Jane, by then her deputy, stepped in to run the school during her absence. The two women spoke daily and met twice a week. A year later Mike and Jane helped her to move to a waterfront apartment and in 2012 she retired. After several interviews, Jane Ashton was appointed headteacher at the school. Following her retirement Pauline had left to live on Crete, visited regularly by the McCarthy family.

Jane curled up on the settee with Mike. Sam was in bed and Georgie was staying out for the night.

Jane said, 'Pauline has invited us over to Crete for Easter.'

'Looks like Paris must wait till summer, a pity.'

'Not really, we can always go in May half-term,' She snuggled up closer to him, 'I'm looking forward to it. Who's this old friend of yours that Georgie and Matt visited in Paris?'

'Oh... Suzanne. I think we'll go and see her when we go. You'll like her.'

'I think you have mentioned her before, years ago, Georgie didn't say much, just that she had made them very welcome and that she was 'dead cool' which I suppose in Georgie-speak is quite a compliment.'

They both smiled and Mike said, 'It's over thirty years since I've seen her, the last time was a couple of years before we met. We send each other the odd letter. I'll drop her a line and tell her we'll come in May, she will be pleased to meet you.' Jane gently pushed her head sleepily into his shoulder.

There was a pause, Mike wanted to ask her the question, which way did she vote. Why he couldn't, he didn't know. He wasn't sure he wanted to know the answer. It was a ridiculous situation to be in, he would just ask...

'Were you and her lovers?'

For a second he was taken aback. He knew that she had asked out of simple curiosity. Jane was the least envious, the least judgemental person he had ever met.

'Yes. I met her on my first trip to Paris, way back in 1979. I was very young, about twenty-one, I think.'

Jane held him close, kissed him gently on the cheek and said, 'Tell me about her.'

He told her everything. Suzanne would have approved.

An hour later a yawning Jane reached over, kissed him, stood up and said, I'm really looking forward to meeting her, she sounds a fascinating lady.' As she ascended the stairs she looked back at him saying, 'I almost forgot, Georgie's left you a note, it's in the kitchen.' Jane went off to bed and Mike went into the kitchen. He sat down at the table and realised he hadn't asked her which way she had voted. It could wait, tomorrow, maybe. Was it really that important after all? At the end of the day we all go into a private booth to vote, that's the essence of democracy, we don't have to tell anyone how we voted. Many things would change when we eventually left the EU but hopefully, democracy will be here to stay. Hopefully...

He saw Georgie's note at the end of the table, reached over and pulled it to him. It was a piece of yellow A4 paper folded in two with the word 'Dad' painted in blue on the front. He opened it and sat down at the table.

Soft or Hard?

In the EU Referendum
Britain voted Out
Still the British people
Don't know what it's about.

There will be negotiations
Which we will have to win
And until that pyrrhic victory
The UK will stay in.

What does Brexit look like?
At what point, will we go?
Government has no answers
No one seems to know.

The Brexit camp claim victory
Was due to their campaign
Yet until this mess is sorted out
Britain will remain.

According to the Government
Brexit can be soft or hard
We can woo the single market
Play the immigration card.

There surely will be trouble
Further on along the track
One thing is for certain though
There is no going back.

Mike smiled to himself. Georgie had written poems since she was at primary school. A couple of years back her poetry had become dark and depressive to the point that her teachers and Jane became worried that she had fallen into a dark phase in her life. They focussed on teenage angst with issues such as self-harming, acne and drug abuse. Mike knew that she was merely reflecting the world around her, as she saw it. He told Jane not to worry, that she would get through it and move on. She had moved on, for the better. The daughter who, like her mother had once ignored anything remotely political had changed. As he went up the stairs he smiled again to himself, at least Brexit was having a positive effect on one member of his family.

Chapter 9
March 2017

Rachel Evans looked down at her notes making little ticks next to the points they had discussed. Occasionally she had written a sub-note next to one or two of the points following a comment Mike had made. This was her method of working, slightly too bureaucratic and ponderous for Mike's liking, yet everyone had their own way. She looked up at the clock and said, 'He will be here in about 20 minutes, could you meet him at reception for me Mike. You have done a wonderful job with this over the past few months and I am forever grateful. GCSE politics will start in September and two years later we will commence the A Level course. I have already decided that you will oversee the Department and that is to your credit. Now, let's go over our visitor's itinerary for the week.'

For the next few minutes they discussed what Sir George Carter's representative from the Ministry of Education would be doing at their school for the next few days. After Rachel had made a few more ticks and notes on the pad in front of her she put the top on her fountain pen and looked up.

'Do you mind if I ask you a slightly personal question?'

For a moment, Mike was wondering where she was heading but said, 'Go ahead.'

'Have you ever thought about going into politics, Mike?'

It was the strangest question she had ever asked him. 'No is the answer. In this country, we have a political party system which is difficult, perhaps impossible to deviate from. I've never been a member of a political party and would need to be so to go into politics. I've never felt strongly enough about one party or the other to join, tending to find faults in both the main ones, including the fringe parties. That doesn't mean I'm not *political* but look on myself more as a commentator on the political system and events.'

She smiled and said, 'That's obviously why Guy Simpson speaks so highly of you, I see the difference between both now. However, what's happened in the United States is incredible, a former TV personality and successful businessman can get to become the most powerful man in the world without having an allegiance to any political party or experience in Government, surely it proves anyone can make it in politics?'

Mike rummaged in his suit jacket pocket and thought for a moment before answering. 'America has a different political system than our own. There are many Independents in Congress who are not allied to a party, it's not called the Land of Opportunity for nothing. However, it's not quite as simple as that, you need a lot of money behind you just to stand as a Presidential candidate, which is usually raised through the party machines. In Donald Trump's case, much of the funding came from his own fortune. I would agree with you that it's incredible, perhaps a phenomenon in his case.'

Rachel was busy making notes. He pulled a piece of paper from his pocket and thought about Guy Simpson. That may explain things, she had spoken in the present tense, he and Rachel obviously kept in touch, interesting and possibly something to do with her 'Politics Project' as Angie sarcastically called it. He still couldn't see what could be in it for Simpson, if anything at all. He looked at the piece of paper with the name Tony Edwards MP written in his handwriting. As Rachel finished writing he said,

'I forgot to tell you, we have a former pupil who is now an MP. Tony Edwards… He was here 20-odd years ago, I thought we might ask him to come and speak to our new politics students, you know, the usual role model stuff. His seat is in the south of England but he might be keen to come back to his old school.'

She paused and looked him straight in the eye.

'Have you contacted him yet?'

'No, it's currently on my list of ideas for next year.'

Rachel put the top on her pen, stood up and brushed down her skirt. She said, 'Leave that one with me, I'll have a think about it.

Don't contact him yet.' She seemed to be lost in thoughts then pulled herself together, looked at the clock and said smiling, 'Our visitor should be arriving about now, pop down and get him for me please Mike.'

Later that day Mike called in to see Stefan Zelinski to arrange a politics presentation to the Year 8 students.

'Hi Stef, I just wanted a chat about another presentation to the Year 8s.'

'Sure, take a seat, cup of tea?'

'Yeah thanks.'

The two men had known each other for a long time and had an easy-going, productive relationship. Stef passed Mike a mug of tea.

'No more problems Stef after those pretty nasty comments following the Brexit vote?'

'Look Mike, I don't blame the kids here, they were just wound up after the vote, I've got a large pair of shoulders, I can take it. It's my kids I worry about, I wouldn't mind, we were all born and raised here, my Mum's from Liverpool, Dad escaped from Poland after the defeat, managed to get to England and fought with the Polish Brigade at Arnhem. Montgomery himself, gave him his medals at the end of the war. We're as English as fish and chips.' He shook his head and laughed a little.

Mike nodded, Brexit had a lot to answer for. Stefan looked at his computer screen. 'I can let you have next Wednesday for the assembly.'

'That's fine, Stef. Do you remember a student called Tony Edwards, was here about twenty years ago?'

Stef shook his head, the name rings a bell, but I can't recall anything, have you got a photo?'

'Maybe, can I use your PC?'

'Sure, go ahead.'

Mike Googled Tony Edwards MP. A picture of a man, late 30s in a grey suit, white shirt and purple tie was prominent on the homepage of the politician's website. Stefan peered at the screen.

'Do you know, he hasn't changed much. I taught geography in those days, he was one of my students. He's obviously done well for himself. I'll tell you something Mike, he was here about the same time as Rachel Evans.'

Georgie was on a reading-week break from college and was busy catching up with her practical assignments at home. She had the use of a spare bedroom, a couple of Mike's old easels and his textbooks. She was working on a pencil copying exercise of one of Modigliani's portraits as Mike looked in.

'Want some company George?'

'Sure, you can give me your opinion on this as well.'

Mike gave her a few tips but he saw she had done a very good job and needed little support. The black, stark eyes of the man in the picture, a trademark of the artist stared back at them.

'It's good George, just keep working on the perspective. Any more trips planned with Matt?'

'Not really, he has a big exam year. Maybe we'll go to Holland in the summer, I'd like to see the galleries in Amsterdam and The Hague just in case we can't do the visits abroad in the third-year due to Brexit.'

She was busy shading the drawing whilst speaking. Mike sat himself on a high stool, watching her as she worked.

'What's the feeling amongst the students about Brexit?'

Georgie looked up, brushed her hair out of her eyes, leaned back in her chair and said,

'We can't believe the attitude of the government, Dad. OK, a small majority in the country voted to leave but nearly half the country didn't. Where are their rights? We know that two groups were responsible for this mess, one, the over-65s and two, the disenfranchised and the forgotten, who might have an excuse of sorts.'

Mike put up his hand and intervened, 'George, you can't say that, not everyone over 65 voted for Brexit and as for people who might feel that politics doesn't represent them or understand their problems, well, it was more likely a protest vote in their case.'

She pulled one leg up underneath her and put down her pencil. She looked at Mike and said quietly, 'Dad, listen, the country is falling to bits over Brexit. The government gives the impression it knows what it's doing when in fact, it hasn't got a clue about how to go about leaving the EU. They go on about a deal with Europe, believe me, they won't get anything at all from Europe. The Europeans, especially the Germans, may well give our people who live in their country citizenship which will cancel out the only bargaining chip our side have, although, to use people as a negotiating device is obscene and disgusting.'

Mike took an intake of breath; Jane was right, his daughter had certainly matured and changed over the past few months.

'When you were in Paris last year, did you by any chance speak to Suzanne about how she felt about Brexit?'

'Of course, Matt and I chatted for ages about it with Suzanne. She can't see things going well for us, says the EU will give us nothing, as a deterrent to any other countries that may be thinking of pulling out. She did say that she wasn't surprised by the result of the Referendum, that she always knew the English would eventually screw up the whole thing.'

Mike nodded, he visualised Suzanne speaking to Georgie and Matt, shrugging and shaking her head. He also knew that she was an Anglophile and wouldn't be judgemental about the British people voting to leave. However, she would be critical of our political leaders for holding a Referendum. She used to joke that when the French had let the people decide things it usually led to the guillotine and the firing squad.

'What about European students at college, what's their view?'

'Same as us, except they are more worried about their future. Many students over the last few years simply haven't gone home after Uni, but stayed on because they love the place. We now have big European communities in this city, Scandinavian, French, Spanish, Greek as well as all the eastern Europeans who live and work here, paying taxes. They assimilate better than in any other city in the country, always have done, that's why we're known as Britain's first multicultural city. Many are my friends... What's going to happen to them, Dad?'

Mike looked down at the floor, for some reason he felt slightly guilty. He couldn't answer her, he had no answer.

Later that evening Mike checked his emails, there was one from Pavel in Croatia. In the summer of 1984 he had spent the six-weeks summer holiday backpacking around Europe by train and bus. He had started in France, gone through Switzerland and Austria and entered Yugoslavia in its autonomous republic of Slovenia. His original intention was to see most of the republics, pass through Albania into Greece and get a flight home. It was the first time he had been in Eastern Europe, although what he found in Yugoslavia surprised and amazed him. He was enthralled by the natural beauty of the country and the people, a proud race of southern Slavs who had fought off invader after invader over the centuries. Most of all he was impressed by the political system and the leader who had put it in place, Josip Broz Tito.

From the very start when he had been waved through at the Austrian border he had been surprised how liberal the communist regime was. He had expected a typical Soviet police state but the whole place seemed as relaxed as Italy or France. He visited Zagreb and Belgrade then took a long, blisteringly hot road journey through the hills to an iconic European city, Sarajevo. Here nestled in a mountainous bowl was a place where east meets west. Mosques and minarets stood next to Christian churches of the Orthodox and Roman faiths and through the centre, and along the river ran an unbroken green line; the route taken on the 28th June 1914 by Franz Ferdinand and his wife in an open-top car. What followed was a botched and farcical assassination by Serb nationalists that the world hardly noticed at the time. At the start and in the final decade of the twentieth century, Sarajevo would forever be associated with the horror and futility of war.

He moved on through stunning mountain scenery where the Partisans had carved Tito's name into hill after hill and on to Montenegro. If he thought that the scenic beauty of Slovenia, Croatia and Bosnia couldn't be surpassed then he was wrong, Montenegro was Europe's hidden gem. From the high limestone peaks and green meadows down to dramatic coastal fjords the tiny republic was breathtakingly beautiful. Later, he discovered that as much as half the population of the country had been wiped out by the Nazis and their allies during the war. At the Albanian border, he was stopped by Yugoslav troops who informed him that the 'Turks', as they called the Albanians, had closed the border and there were occasional artillery exchanges. Time was moving on and he was running short of money. He headed up the coast towards Dubrovnik.

A few miles outside the walled city his bus stopped to drop off some passengers at a small fishing village called Cavtat. Having been informed that he could take a boat into Dubrovnik, he decided to have a look around. He wandered into a café, dumped his rucksack and asked the tall bartender in English did he know anywhere he could stay. The barman reached for a key and asked Mike to follow him. He was taken to a small stone cottage nearby where the man introduced himself as Pavel Bozic. After he had gone Mike looked in the mirror. He didn't immediately recognise his own image. His face was mahogany brown, his hair long and matted. Pavel would later joke with him that when he first saw him he thought he was an Australian backpacker and had walked all the way from the outback.

He stayed in Cavtat for the next ten days before Pavel drove him to Dubrovnik airport and found an attractive stewardess from the state airline that regularly flew tourists to and from the United Kingdom. After a short conversation during which Pavel passed something to her she told Mike to check in with her at the desk. Three hours later he was on a plane bound for Manchester.

Mike and Pavel had stayed friends since their first meeting. During the war in the 1990s, Dubrovnik and Cavtat were shelled by Serb forces. Pavel's sister had been killed and his café destroyed. He went to live as a refugee in Vienna where the year before Georgie was born Mike and Jane visited him. He later returned to Croatia and was currently working as a guide in Dubrovnik showing tourists from cruise ships the delights of the city.

Mike opened his email.

Hello Michael,

First, an apology. I was a bit unkind to you in my last couple of emails. I found it incredulous that the UK could vote to leave the EU. You will know that my people had been through hell, first in 1914-18. Then in the Second War and then again in the 1990s. We were never able to choose our own destiny until now. We never knew till now how wonderful it was to go to the voting place and not have men who were your enemy watching every move you made and who you voted for. Most of the time we were not allowed to vote anyway. I was upset when you voted for Brexit because I knew that England never had to live under the whip, the concentration camp and the firing squad so the English could never understand why people in Europe should embrace the EU so much.

We took the opportunity that God had given us with both hands to join the European Union. We are now an independent country and a member of the EU and as a people, never been happier. Hundreds of years of slavery, murder and domination by Rome, Venice, Vienna, Istanbul, Berlin and Belgrade have now been swept away and with the support of the EU we are a proud, prosperous nation.

I was a little bit bad-tempered when I heard what your country had done and I know you will know that. Now, I can see things differently. You too have a proud history, so much different from ours. Now, my temper has been replaced by worry, for you and your people. Your people are my special favourites, I have a place in my heart for you all. We hear so many stories about Brexit, as you call it, about how things might get bad again in Ireland. How your economy might collapse. How Scotland might leave your country. I don't know what to believe any more. Because of this I would so much like to hear your views, I know you will tell me the truth Mike. You will tell me how it really is. I am so worried that this Brexit could be your Sarajevo.

Your friend, Pavel

Mike had long since forgiven his friend for his previous emails, although in truth there was nothing to forgive. He remembered television reports from the war which showed shells landing in Cavtat and inside Dubrovnik's walls. It was impossible at the time to get any news of Pavel and his family. Phone links were either restricted or disabled by the opposing forces, besides, for all he knew the population could have abandoned the town, fled to Dubrovnik or even taken to the hills to fight as their people had always done. It was a civil war, the worst type; no mercy would be expected, or given. Mike could understand Pavel's views completely about Britain leaving the EU. His homeland had been devastated by war and suffering since Roman times and he and his people were now proud to be an independent, peaceful country within the European Union. More importantly, it's their choice. Things were different for the British. Every nation had its own unique culture and history which reflected how they went about doing things. He would reply to him that he would like to visit him in Croatia where they could chat about Brexit and old times and show Jane and the children Cavtat, a place which held so many happy memories for him. He mulled over the final sentence of Pavel's email... *Brexit could be your Sarajevo.*

A week later Mike called into see Rachel Evans for their weekly meeting. Ten minutes earlier he had received a text message from a local radio station asking if he could be available for a lunchtime visit to the studio for another Brexit debate. He had taken part in two earlier programmes at the same station but would ask Rachel for her permission.

'Yes, that's no problem Mike, you are free today, you must be something of a fixture at their studio.'

Mike smiled and shook his head. 'I'm afraid fame has come late in life.'

She reached for her notebook and passed a sheet of paper across to him.

'It's a letter from Sir George at the Department thanking us for looking after his representative and wishing us well for the future. I'll send you a copy for your records.'

Mike read over the document. It was the standard civil service letter on cream embossed paper. At midpoint the writer wished his thanks to be conveyed to Mr Michael McCarthy 'for his sterling work in supporting your project, my best wishes go to him as he embarks upon his new role.'

Mike smiled. He could just imagine old Sir George dictating that out loud to his secretary. He finished reading down to the final line, '... and Rachel, I want to personally wish you well on your chosen journey, you are a credit to your profession.'

Mike looked at that line a couple of times before handing the letter back to Rachel.

'Well done Mike, for everything. I want to thank you again, personally for all your hard work and mainly for your support to me.' She beamed at him, no more notes, no more trips to London. He was pleased yet something remained to be asked.

'Rachel, do you mind if I ask you something?'

She looked searchingly at him. 'Yes of course, ask away.' She smiled.

'I can't help thinking that you aren't telling me something. Something I think that's relevant to all the work we have done over the last few months.'

Rachel had turned her chair and was looking out of the window. She sighed, stood up and said, 'It's a lovely spring day. Let's go for a walk outside.'

Mike knew most of the staff at the radio station, he sipped at his coffee whilst adjusting his headphones as music played in the background. Across the banks of equipment, he watched the presenter. To his left sat one of his old adversaries from the school debate last year, the local councillor and politician from the Labour party, Jack Nelson. Fifteen minutes earlier they had shaken hands and chatted informally about Mike's TV appearance and subjects such as football and holidays. Mike wasn't taken in by the cheery bonhomie on offer, Nelson was just about the toughest cookie around the local political scene. A survivor of the 1980s when he had appeared regularly on demonstrations, picket lines and strike committees, he had recently tapped into a new political mood in the city, far more populist than confrontational. He was a committed Brexiteer yet to his credit had managed to retain his popularity amongst the local public. Jack Nelson was a clever and tricky customer, this wasn't going to be easy.

The producer had gone through the format of the show with both men. There was no studio audience on this occasion, each man would answer phone-in questions from members of the public for around 30 minutes. The music finished and the presenter gave both men a thumbs-up signal indicating that the phone-in was about to start. The debate went well for Mike for the first 20 minutes, many of the callers agreed with his views that we needed to stay in the Single Market and not restrict immigration from the European Union. Some disagreed with Mike, yet after giving his argument he told them that he respected their views, however, they would have to agree to disagree. The presenter then introduced a student called Gill.

'Hello Gill, you're through to Mike McCarthy, let's hear your question for him.'

'Isn't the whole European project finished and not before time. It's a haven for bankers and overpaid bureaucrats who don't give a damn for the ordinary people of Europe and the world. It's allied to the defence industries of Britain, France, Italy, Germany and Sweden and an arm of NATO. The EU will sell arms to anyone, including regimes with very dodgy human rights' records, especially in the Middle East, to kill and maim children.' As she spoke Mike glanced at Nelson who was nodding away in agreement.

'Hi Gill. First, I am not here to defend countries who sell arms to, as you put it, dodgy regimes. The EU has an excellent human rights' record, so, as far as arms sales are concerned your point should be directed towards individual governments who negotiate and sell arms to those regimes. As to your other point about bankers, I was here in the 1980s when this city had reached the lowest point of its history. Unemployment in some areas was as high as 65%, the place was losing its population in the hundreds of thousands, bleeding away daily to London, the Midlands and Europe. It wasn't safe to walk the streets and our magnificent Georgian buildings were either boarded up or falling to pieces. Things got so bad that even the schoolchildren went on strike to protest at what was happening. The only body prepared to help Liverpool recover from this catastrophe was the European Union and their money, or bankers, as you put it. It was EU money that rebuilt this city, that's why on 23rd June last year, we voted Remain.' There was cheering in the background of wherever Gill was speaking from.

Nelson was shouting, 'Rubbish, let me answer that!' He was being waved away by the presenter who seized his chance, saying, 'Gill, where are you? Who are all those people I can hear? Can you put someone else on to speak please?' Gill was saying that she was in the Students' Union with lots of others who were listening to the debate. Suddenly a male voice came on the phone, 'That guy Mike is right, the Conservatives under Margaret Thatcher had all but destroyed the people of this city, they had nowhere else to go but Europe. It was the same in my own city, Sheffield.'

Now Jack Nelson was shouting into his microphone, 'But Sheffield voted to leave, come on, let me come back on this.' The presenter relented and let him speak.

'I don't need a history lesson from Mr McCarthy, in fact, I'm going to give him one.'

He was looking directly at Mike, his eyes bulging.

'While he and his liberal-elite mates were living the Life of Riley at university and no doubt voting for the SDP, I was out on the streets of this city fighting back against the wreckers at Westminster, out to destroy us. How dare he suggest for one second that the bankers in Europe helped us out, they are only interested in their own bank accounts in Switzerland and Monaco. Look what they've done to Greece!'

The producer had slipped quietly into the studio, had a quiet word with the presenter and stood with his arms folded looking at Nelson and Mike. The presenter, looking seriously worried said 'Jack, I'm going to let Mike answer those things you have said.' He was indicating that they were still broadcasting live. Mike and Jack Nelson sat facing each other, just three feet apart. Mike sighed and said quietly.

'In the 1980s I wasn't at university, I wasn't living it up and voting for the SDP, as Jack has said. I was working as a teacher in a run-down part of Liverpool trying to help kids who hardly had enough to eat because Dad had lost his job and Mum was usually bombed off her head with despair and tranquilisers. When some of my pupils came to me and said they wanted to try and do something to help by going on strike, I shook my head and laughed, then wished them good luck as they marched off with their banners towards the Town Hall.'

The producer was looking interested now, gesturing to the presenter to keep things going. Jack Nelson was breathing heavily, red faced. Mike McCarthy continued speaking into the microphone.

'Nothing had ever been seen like it before, or since, for that matter. School children on strike against the policies of their own government. Of course, no one quite knew how to respond, not least the schools. Myself and another teacher were told to follow them but on no account to join in with them. We followed them all the way to the Town Hall where they met up with hundreds of other kids from all over the city. It was a surreal situation, even the police didn't know what to do and just stood around smiling and laughing. The whole thing was good-natured and I suppose, typical of that crazy time. We had experienced riots, strikes, demonstrations, depopulation, mass unemployment and now this, which at least was peaceful and amusing. A few of the older kids went to the doors of the building to try to get access to the council meeting which was taking place inside and the doors were slammed shut in their faces by an usher and… Jack Nelson.'

The next ten seconds seemed later to pass very slowly. Jack Nelson shot to his feet slamming down his earphones on the table. Both producer and presenter instantly reached for switches cutting the transmission off the air. Nelson launched himself at Mike who had stood up, taking a few steps backwards to prevent physical contact. Two security men were grappling with Jack Nelson and coffee cups were sent flying.

Later that evening Mike sat alone listening to Schubert's C Major Quintet. It was music to reflect to, something he found himself doing more and more frequently. Jack Nelson wasn't a bad sort and later actually apologised for his behaviour. They had both gone and sat in a reception area adjacent to the studio, the staff bringing them coffee. Mike had been well prepared for Jack's personal attacks and had even brought along a blared newspaper photograph of him in shirtsleeves, arms folded, looking out of the glass Town Hall doors at the kids, like a nightclub bouncer, a profession he had once practised in his younger days. There had been no need to show him the photograph, his reaction had said everything.

Nelson explained to Mike that that they were expecting some sort of assault on the council chamber by the police or the army, that they were all being watched by the Special Branch and MI5 and half expected to be detained and held without trial at any time. He went on to say that they were very difficult and dangerous times, the IRA had tried to wipe out the government with a single bomb in Brighton, Britain was being ripped apart with riots and disorder, that we could easily have slipped into civil war. When the kids appeared outside the Town Hall he and others honestly believed it was some sort of stunt by the authorities to keep them occupied while others stormed the building from the back. He started to cheer up saying that they should have taken the children inside, made a fuss of them, got the TV cameras in and let them be interviewed. He laughed, saying that would have done more for their cause than riots and revolution.

Mike had said on air that it had been a crazy time and so it was. The Liverpool School Children's Strike had gone down in local folklore; if ever it was mentioned at his school students and younger staff were disbelieving, until of course they reached for their phones and googled the subject. Was Jack Nelson exaggerating about Special Branch surveillance, detentions and civil war? Perhaps, but perhaps not, we lived in a very different world altogether during the 1980s. It was sometimes difficult for younger people to understand just how bad things had been in those days. Just a few months later he had found himself standing on a rooftop in Berlin looking down at something as incredulous as it was evil and deadly. No riots there, nothing as innocuous as kids walking out of school, just plain old dictatorship, torture and death. In 1989, at the end of a decade when the Cold War had heated up and threatened to blow the world apart, after his own country had changed forever, he watched as countless thousands of people stormed up, over and through the deadliest barrier on earth. He had looked for her of course but there were too many people. Some had been picked out in the lights, standing atop the Wall but he never saw her. She would have been there, along with all the others. Where would they go, what would they and millions more turn to as the old order collapsed around them? They had only one thing they could turn to, the European Union.

Jane walked into the room in a long white dressing gown, recently showered. She slid up next to him on the settee, like she had first done so, back in the mid '80s. She kissed his cheek gently saying,

'Are you coming to bed?'

Mike said, 'Yes,' then in a quiet voice added,

'Jane, which way did you vote in the Referendum?'

Chapter 10
April 2017

He liked airports. He didn't like flying. He sat drinking a coffee, feeling younger. It was a long time since he had travelled abroad alone, without Jane, without the children. His school had broken up a couple of days later at Easter than Jane and Sam's who had already left to be with Pauline on Crete. It was a strange but not unpleasant feeling, a return to his youth except travel today was busier, sanitised, impersonal and usually on time. He had about 40 minutes before he needed to go to his gate so he downed his coffee and went for a walk. His flight from Manchester to Crete would take four hours so he went and bought three current affairs magazines to keep him occupied on the flight. He put them in his bag and headed to a seat to kill time.

He sat thinking about the past few weeks. He had written to Suzanne who was delighted he was bringing Jane to see her, 'after all these years.' Perhaps a slight touch of sarcasm there, entirely in keeping. She was effusive about Georgie and Matt saying she had no worries about England with young people like them. She had also insisted that they must stay with her, that she would start to get things ready and they had a lot to talk about. He had told Jane everything about their relationship including the fact that it had continued when he had next visited Paris. Mike didn't hide anything from her, it was pointless. Jane had listened carefully then said, 'You were both young and very obviously in love. You were right for her at that time and she was right for you.' That was typical of Jane, pragmatic and understanding just as she had been two weeks ago, when he had asked her the question about the Referendum.

She had told him that she had abstained and explained why.

During the Referendum campaign, she had seen her 14-year-old son become worried and concerned about the outcome, her daughter out most nights at debates and rallies, but most of all she had seen the effects on her husband, who had become obsessed with everything surrounding the whole thing, before, during and afterwards. She had no intention of increasing the tension in her household. He had sat speechless for a few minutes then turned towards her and suggested that they go to bed. Over the following days, he had felt like an extraordinarily heavy weight had been lifted from his shoulders.

She had been right of course. He had once viewed abstention as a form of cowardice, a cop out and the excuse of the ill-informed, devious and apathetic. Jane hadn't voted for the best of reasons, the welfare of her family. Maybe he had become obsessed with the whole Referendum and Brexit thing and the near descent into violence with Jack Nelson proved it. He didn't blame Nelson for the spat, he blamed himself. He was the one who had done his research on Jack Nelson's past and gambled correctly that he would react the way he did. But let's be honest who doesn't have a past and a few skeletons in the cupboard? He was no saint himself, none of us were.

The walk around the school yard with Rachel Evans had also paled into insignificance. She had told him that she was considering going into parliamentary politics. This hadn't come as a great surprise to Mike, there were a few subtle pointers that he had picked up on over the last few months. She had asked him his opinion so he gave it. He told her that it was her choice, that only she could decide whether it was the right decision after careful consideration and consultation. He told her that she was a good communicator, an excellent public-speaker and possessed a natural ability to engage and utilise the media. She had smiled at the last point, they both did, nothing else needed to be said on that. Mike also suggested to her that in his opinion she would be better building up towards the next General Election, By-elections can focus all the media's attention in one place, in a General Election she would be one amongst thousands of candidates across the country, besides it would give her more time to prepare. He finally asked her what party she had decided upon. She told him that she hadn't decided yet. He had laughed and said that currently it probably didn't matter too much. He decided not to ask her anything more about Tony Edwards MP, she would have enough on her plate over the next couple of years and might be sitting next to him or opposite him in 2020. He checked the screen and it was time to go to his gate.

The plane levelled and the seatbelt sign went off. Mike got to his feet, opened the overhead locker and took the three magazines, an iPod and earphones from his bag. He settled down, put on some music and started flicking through the magazines. All the covers had a large '50' on the cover indicating that Article 50 had been triggered by the British government. There were the usual predictions of gloom and doom during the forthcoming Brexit negotiations along with the problems facing Donald Trump's Administration as it went towards the 100 days in office milestone. Most observers were warning of an eventual clash with North Korea, something which could lead to a regional war. Mike hoped not. The European news was focussing on the forthcoming French election and he wondered which candidate Suzanne would be supporting. Knowing her, none of them. He finally settled on a long article about Alternative Facts, Post-Trust and Fake News, all phrases that had entered our vocabulary over the previous year.

An hour later he tried to stretch his legs but had cramp. He stood up, dropping his magazines. He thought about Orson Welles's famous quip about flying being a mixture of Fear and Boredom; how right he was, except he forgot one, Discomfort. In the big fella's case, it obviously wasn't a problem, he could just imagine Citizen Kane lounging back in a huge wicker chair surrounded by cushions, a stunning Rita Heyworth in an Imperial Airlines uniform pouring out Scotch for him, attending to his Fear and Boredom. He reached down from his seat to pick up the open magazine and his eye was immediately drawn to a photograph of a woman.

Initially, there was some recognition, but he was still unsure. She had short, ash-blonde hair and wore fashionable glasses along with a smart dark suit jacket and white blouse. It was the smile that gave her away and a quick look at the text confirmed it beyond doubt. He began to read.

Germany
Return of a Maverick

There's a scene in one of Hollywood's old Westerns when the bad boy returns to town after a period of exile, walks in the saloon bar, orders a drink from a terrified bartender, turns to the worried looking townsfolk and plays with his gun. The Maverick had returned and things would now be different around these parts.

Last week a well-known Maverick returned to centre stage of German politics. Maria Schenk, one time youngest member of the unified Bundestag, an enfant terrible of the Social Democrats, held a rally outside the small Town Hall of her Berlin constituency where she declared that Germany had made a big mistake in taking in the recent wave of immigrants from the Middle East and now had to 'redefine' its role within the European Union. One could visualise the SPD bigwigs with their heads in their hands, quoting the song from The Sound of Music, *'How do you solve a problem like Maria?'*

The redoubtable Ms Schenk is no stranger to stunts and over the years has developed the U-turn into a political tool. She first came to note in the early 90s as the youngest national elected representative of a recently unified Germany and was even seen as a future leader of the SPD. She quickly made her mark by taking politics to the streets. Her most famous 'Strassepolitik' was a protest to obtain the best drugs and medical care available for Aids patients. She dressed 50 men and women from a local theatre group in hospital gowns and laid them in the road outside Berlin's largest hospital. It turned out that her brother had died of an Aids-related disease. No less a person than Helmut Kohl, whilst disapproving, called the act 'remarkable'. Later she campaigned for the government to release people's Stasi files only to change her mind when a man in Dresden stabbed to death his neighbour when he found out he'd been spying on him for years. Her political enemies jumped on her U-turn suggesting she may have her own Stasi file. No stranger to the German tabloid press, in 1998 it was revealed that she had been having an affair with a married member of an opposition party. When reporters besieged her apartment, she told them that it was a 'true and lasting' relationship. The following day she ended the affair.

For the last few years she has been relatively quiet, some saying she has been writing her memoirs, other's speculating that she had changed and another saying sarcastically she had 'grown up'. It seems they spoke too soon, with a General Election this year in Germany it looks as though a political Maverick has returned. Things could well be different around these parts.

Mike read the article three times. He was shocked at the death of Karl-Heinz and bewildered by Maria. Being bewildered by Maria was nothing new to him, he had found out the hard way about her personal U-turns. It appeared that she was still acting erratically; on the one hand staging a noble, if dramatic political event to help and support those afflicted by HIV, on the other, a rather squalid little affair that she would have been better saying nothing about to the press. Maria, saying nothing, not possible. Why should he defend her? He wasn't, he was long past that. He looked again at her photograph. Her wonderful smile had always been her trademark and she had gone to look more like Karl as she had aged. He tried to work out how old she was, early 50s at the most. It seems she had blown a very fine political career, something she would have excelled at with her natural confidence and intelligence. It was Karl-Heinz he kept thinking about, the unanswered letters, the supposed move to Switzerland, giving up his law firm. It must have been a terrible time for him, Maria and their mother; thinking back Maria adored him, he was her big brother, her idol and role model. That business with the people lying down in the road outside the hospital was vintage Maria and Karl would have quietly approved, after very gently telling her off. Mike was devastated by the news, hurt and deeply upset.

Pauline met him at the airport, Jane and Sam taking the opportunity to get some sun at Pauline's villa. The drive from Heraklion took about an hour and they took the opportunity to speak on the way.

Pauline was smiling as they drove out of the airport. 'I hear you locked horns with old Jack Nelson.'

'It wasn't really like that Pauline, we ended up the best of friends afterwards.'

'I remember Jack from the old days, back in the 70s. He was always an angry bugger, out on the streets fighting with the coppers when the dock strikes were on. He sounds like he's still at it.'

'No, I think he's changed a bit, he was a man of his time, we're all shaped by our past but as we get older we look back and wonder if it was all worth it.'

Pauline glanced at him and said. 'That's very philosophical, Michael. So, you have a beautiful wife, two fantastic children a pretty good standard of living and you wonder if it's been worth it?'

He smiled. 'You forgot to mention a fabulous friend, mentor and the older sister I never had. Someone I have always been able to turn to when things got rough... Shall I go on? Anyway, I've had enough of politics, Brexit, Alternative Facts, Fake News, Article 50, the whole bloody lot.'

She headed out onto the main road which led west from the city.

'Michael, I have known you for 30 years. The day we met you told me how you'd climbed up next to the Berlin Wall to get a better look, been involved in demonstrations in Paris and as a boy stood next to your father at political meetings. I know you, it's in the blood, you might go off occasionally to think it over but you'll always come back to it. You know I'm right.'

He did. Pauline knew what he was like, perhaps more than Jane. The magazine article had shaken him. The death of Karl-Heinz, Maria, throwing away all her principles, apparently turning away from the European ideal, something she had infused in him. Upon reflection, he had been in love with something in Berlin, the city, yes, without doubt, from a time and place or as the locals would say, the zeitgeist, it had no equals. Maria? He wasn't sure, or was he deluding himself? It's always the hurt partner who insists they weren't in love. In a pique, he had thrown the magazine into a rubbish bag as the stewardess made her rounds on the plane, now he wished he hadn't.

Jane gave him a huge hug when they arrived, Sam was in the swimming pool and Mike waved to him from the kitchen. It was always good to see Jane and Pauline together, they chatted away as if they had never been apart as they began to prepare dinner. Pauline's neighbours Eamon and Costas had been invited to dinner. The McCarthy family had met them on several occasions, Eamon was a retired bookseller from Dublin and Costas had moved to the area from eastern Crete where he had sold his two tavernas in a busy tourist area. Sam dried off and joined Mike in the living room.

'How was the flight, Dad?'

'Oh, all right I suppose, you know I'm not the best flyer around Sam.'

'What happens next with Brexit? Will we have to pay all that money to the EU. Some of my friends at school think they are trying to rip us off Dad.'

Mike wasn't sure what to say to Sam so trod carefully.

'Well, it's going to take some time Sam, at least two years, so we'll get a good idea of how it unfolds as the talks go along.' Sam didn't look the least bit impressed by the answer and left to have a shower. Mike was thinking about the magazine article, he had tried to put it out of his mind but couldn't. Jane didn't know about Maria. She knew he had been in Berlin the year before they had met and when she had asked him about it he had told her that the place was interesting, damaged and divided, perhaps forever. Pauline and Bob had asked him more questions when they had met socially but he was just as reticent. Bob had suggested that it must have been a sobering experience for him, especially crossing into East Berlin. It was a perceptive Pauline who had looked at him knowingly. She always knew when he was trying to hide something. With the passage of time and the fall of the Wall, Berlin had faded from other people's minds. For Mike, it had always been there, in the background; the bitterest and sweetest of memories, today had pushed that time back to front of his consciousness.

Dinner was a welcome relief from his thoughts. Pauline was in fine form, making them all laugh, as only she could. Eamon and Costas were both a few years older than Pauline, both widowers, Costas, portly, smiling, quietly wise. Eamon, tall, thin, entertaining, the perfect complement to Pauline. After dinner, Sam had gone into the living room deep into himself, phone in hands. Jane and Pauline began to clear up and Costas clapped his hands as the hostess returned with a bottle of five star Greek brandy and glasses, Jane bringing plates of sliced fruit to the table.

It was Eamon who got the conversation going.

'Now, tell us all about this Brexit business Michael, or as I keep calling it, Breakfast!'

There was the usual laughter from everyone before Mike said, 'There's not much to say about it anymore, Article 50 has been triggered, we're on our way out, that's about it really.'

Pauline, with a mischievous look said. 'Now, that doesn't sound like the man who I watched on television the day after the Referendum and if I could get it here in Crete it must have been seen across the world.' She gestured to Eamon and Costas, 'Gentlemen, we have at our table no less than Mr Mike McCarthy, that famous, international politics pundit!'

They were all clapping, including Jane who was smiling at him across the table. Mike was embarrassed for a moment before Costas said quietly, 'Michael, I too saw this TV programme, you were very good, a true expert.' Eamon chipped in, 'Ah... The English are good with the words Costas, they've been kidding everyone for centuries, look at that Shakespeare fella.' Everyone was laughing again including Mike. Pauline, on her feet pouring out brandy for them said, 'Eamon O'Reilly, the Irish know one or two things themselves about words but what you don't like to admit is the Scots taught you everything you know.' There was laughter again, Pauline and Eamon's good-natured Celtic banter was a common feature at these get togethers, Mike felt upbeat and better than he had for months.

They all wanted to know how he had ended up doing a television show. He told them that it had been a gamble by Guy Simpson who had been plunged into it himself with just a few hours' notice. Broadcasting from Liverpool it had been difficult to get hold of senior politicians and pundits as most were down in London and would have been needed during the night and the following day. Originally, it had been planned as a low-key radio show with the expectation that the Remain camp would win. Once it became clear that Leave had won the producers were asked to put together a TV programme. They sent over the crews from Manchester who set everything up in a short space of time. Simpson had hosted their school Referendum debate and phoned the school asking if Mike could be made available.

Everyone was serious now and commenting. Pauline said, 'The setting looked fantastic, cruise ships in the river, the marvellous buildings, lovely sunshine.'

Costas said, 'I have never been to Liverpool but I agree with Pauline, it looked incredible on the television. When I first turned on I thought it was an American city, it looked so impressive.'

Mike told Costas and Eamon that the waterfront was now one of the most recognisable places in the world, in fact it was a World Heritage site, much in demand for film and television productions. Guy Simpson and his producers knew they were on a winner with the backdrop.

Jane had been sitting quietly looking admiringly at Mike and said, 'Guy Simpson has never looked back since that day, pops up on lots of political programmes these days. I'm making coffee, anyone want one?' Jane left and Pauline joined her.

Eamon said to Mike, 'So, what's next for you, more television?'

'No, I'm finished with all that now Eamon. I did two or three radio shows but I've had enough. It's back to school for me.' He smiled. 'I could do a hundred radio shows but it's not going to change the fact that we are leaving the EU. I just need to get on with my life now.'

The two women had taken their coffee into the living room, the men staying in the kitchen, Mike drinking coffee, Costas and Eamon, brandy. Mike said to them, 'Why don't you two tell me what you think about Brexit, it would be good to get an opinion from the rest of Europe for a change.'

It was Eamon who answered first.

'I have to tell you Mike, I think the whole thing will be a disaster for the British. People are concerned about Northern Ireland, what's going to happen with the border with the Republic? Scotland have voted to hold another Independence Referendum and are causing trouble, they might want away. Now there's a problem with Gibraltar, who knows where that will lead. If Brussels gets its way you'll be hit with a hefty bill well before any negotiations take place. No one from Europe will trade with you and to top it all what's going to happen to all your people who live and work on the continent, not to mention the Europeans resident in Britain. And here was me thinking it was just the Irish that usually made an unholy mess of things. At least those boys in Dublin put a clause in their Referendums that if the result isn't in the best interests of the Irish people the government can take no notice of it. Now there's democracy for you, bunch of comedians.'

Eamon and Mike laughed while Costas sat back, playing with a set of yellow wooden beads that Greek men traditionally ran through their fingers whilst thinking. Last year he had given Jane a beautiful set of some sort of semi-precious stones. He was nodding as both men spoke and Mike was keen to hear what he had to say.

'Costas, what about the Greeks? Your country has had a difficult time lately, so, are the European Union heroes or villains?'

Costas was playing with the beads, deep in thought. In his quiet voice, he said.

'The European Union is an empire. It may do things a little differently from other empires but it is one, just the same. In every empire, there will be a dominant nation, whether it has been the Greeks, Persians, Romans, Turks and Russians.' He smiled at Mike and said, 'even the British.' In the case of the EU it is currently Germany. I say currently because even in its short history the EU has had two dominant nations, first France, then the Germans.'

'There are two big problems for empires; one are the small, weak nations who crave independence at any cost, usually by force. The second is more complicated but deadlier. This is when a powerful partner nation or group of nations sees itself as the dominant power but cannot, for whatever reasons take the top role. It then decides to go it alone, historically with catastrophic results for both sides. When the Roman Empire split in such a way, both sides were weaker, first the west, including Rome itself fell to the Barbarians.

The eastern provinces, centred on Constantinople were stronger but were eventually swallowed up by new powers and empires that arose. Many of the current problems in Europe, including Greece's can be traced back to that split.'

He paused, looked down, played with the tassel on the beads then said. 'Does that last point remind you of any particular country Michael?'

It was Eamon who answered. 'My little homeland comes into the first category Costas.' They all smiled and Mike said, 'Yes, I agree up to a point Costas, but surely when we live in a modern democracy you can't afford to disregard the views of the minority, in this case the 48% who voted to remain.'

'Ah… Now we are talking politics Michael! I'm afraid in a democracy the victor helps himself to the spoils, however close the result. However, a close result can cause serious problems in any democracy, it inevitably causes a split to occur when the victor does not take the views of the loser into account. Unfortunately, they have a habit of not doing so. Take it from me, from the country who invented this word, this concept, democracy. Every political system, including, no… especially democracy, is open to abuse. We Greeks know all about dictatorships that masquerade as democracies, both ancient and modern. I will give you only one piece of advice my friend. Ask yourself if you can do anything about it, if the answer is no, then don't try to. If the answer is yes, then do what you have to do.'

Mike listened carefully to what Costas said. He was particularly impressed by what he had said right at the end.

Mike looked out of the window towards the swimming pool. Jane was lying on a sun lounger in a bikini, a straw hat pulled down over her eyes. He looked at her admiringly, she had kept her slim, willowy figure and her blonde, English-rose looks. He made a mental note to tell her to be careful in the sun. Pauline had taken Sam to a new shopping precinct near Chania, the largest town nearest to her home. He poured soda water into two glasses of orange juice with ice, picked them up, went outside and sat next to her.

161

Jane sat up taking a sip of her drink. 'How did your little chat with Eamon and Costas go last night Mike?'

'All right, the usual blarney from Eamon, he was in good form. Costas was his old, philosophical self, except the world has turned full circle since we were last here. Brexit has had a knock-on effect on the whole world, look at America, parts of Europe. Despite what we may think of ourselves everyone still looks to us for a lead. If something happens in the United Kingdom the world sits up and takes notice. We saw it recently when parliament was attacked, the shock was real, yet look at all the many genuine messages of support from everywhere. It's as if they knew that if something like that can happen in England with all its ancient, solid stability it could happen anywhere. We saw the best of our people that day and afterwards. I've always been the first to criticise and have a dig at our parliamentarians but they set an example to us all and we responded together. You see Jane, first and foremost I'm a patriot, proud to be an Englishman and a European.'

He suddenly realised something and said. 'Oh... I'm sorry, I promised you I was finished with Brexit and everything else to do with it.'

She leaned towards him, touched his cheek and smiled. 'Michael, do you think for one minute that I want you to change? I love you the way you are, the way you always have been. When we first met, you taught me everything that I didn't know about Europe, politics and, basically, about someone called Mike McCarthy. I loved you then and I love you now. Don't ever change. I think the best thing for you and me would be to put back the clock 30-odd years and revisit the places you went to when you were young. We're starting with Paris, lets continue with some of the other places.'

She kissed him on the cheek and said. 'The hire car we ordered will be here after lunch, let's go for a drive together.'

He smiled and stood up saying he would look forward to it.

As he walked away she called him back. She took something from her bag and handed it to him. It was a set of Greek worry beads.

'Costas gave them to me, for you.'

He smiled. That was typical of Costas.

He sat on a stone bench looking out to sea. The sun was starting to dip making the air pleasantly cool. He could see Jane in the distance, her light-blue dress flapping slightly in the breeze. Occasionally she would remove her wide-brimmed hat and bend down to take a closer look. Graves, again. On the first and most of his other journeys around the continent he had come across row after row of stone slabs marking the site of death of thousands of men and women who had been slaughtered for some cause or other. This was the German cemetery. They had visited the British war cemetery earlier that afternoon and as they were leaving an old Greek man who was lovingly tending the graves urged them to go and visit this site. Young men from two European nations who had died fighting each other on the soil of another European country.

They had believed what they were doing was right, that they couldn't be mistaken about their cause. We can all feel the same way about our causes. James and Jean-Michel had undoubtedly felt the same as they fought together against overwhelming odds throughout France. He himself had felt a measure of the hatred that comes about when fellow Europeans build walls and anti-tank barriers and fortify them with machine-gun posts simply to stop their fellow countrymen seeing each other. It was dangerous to believe that World War Two was an end to it all: it spawned the Cold War and a real danger of complete annihilation. The people of Northern Ireland and Britain had fought a savage war of attrition for almost 40 years and in the final decade of the century a quarter of a million people died in Yugoslavia, a conflict that saw the worst excesses of all the other wars of a divided and hideous century. After a period of relative peace and an attempt to reconcile differences by building unity of sorts were the first cracks appearing and would we return to the sins of the past? Only time would tell. Maybe he shouldn't give up his personal fight, perhaps there was something he could do about Brexit after all, there was a long way to go yet.

Jane walked back uphill and sat on the bench next to him.

'Some of these poor boys were only the same age as Georgie, just a few years older than Sam.'

Mike said nothing.

Mike was getting his latest dose of Boredom, Fear and Discomfort. They were still an hour out from Manchester and he was tired, hungry and stiff. That morning Eamon had called to Pauline's to wish them a safe journey and stayed for an hour chatting with Mike whilst Jane packed. He told Mike that he had greatly enjoyed their little get-together the other night and had been thinking about things since.

'You know Michael, I think this Brexit business has a lot to do with nostalgia. You see, many people in both our countries crave for a time long past. I remember well the old Dublin of the 1950s, the smell of the men's pipe tobacco, the hops from the Guinness factory, the sea water and the incense from the churches. My father's old bookshop with the signed picture of James Joyce shaking hands with Daddy back in the twenties. Nuns and priests walking across St Stephen's Green, the accordion music coming from the pubs. We hardly had two pennies to rub together but it was a grand time, or so we thought. If people could vote to return to that they would do so tomorrow. It's nonsense of course, your memory only allows you certain pleasurable thoughts, it doesn't remind me of the filthy kids begging in bare feet on O'Connell Street, the stink of the slums down by the docks, the beatings by a sadistic teacher who was drunk most of the time, the prostitutes everywhere and the violence dished out by the Peelers most Saturday nights.'

Mike listened, fascinated by Eamon's theory.

'It's the same with your country Michael. Most of the older ones who voted to leave were hoping for a return to the glory days of Empire, factories that produced the best of everything and sent it across the world, full employment, hospitals with just a few patients, picnics on the beaches, holidays in Cornwall, church on Sundays and football played by Englishmen who caught the bus to the match and had a few jars with the fans afterwards. I could go on and on. It will never exist again, never really did in the first place, but just the thought of it and some smooth-tongued bugger on TV every night promising them their dream was just enough to swing it to the Leave lot.'

He smiled saying, 'You don't come out of things too rosy either

164

Michael, or rather the Remain side. The case you put up was frankly, abysmal. Your main spokespersons were members of a ruling elite who couldn't even agree with each other, you were as bad as the other side for selling a dream, in your case some sort of European utopia where everything was sweetness and light. You should have been telling people about the damage to the economy, the increased threat of terrorism, the lack of public investment in health and schools, unemployment and the banks and car factories pulling out if people voted Leave. Instead the other side stole your clothes, turned it on its head and used all those points in their argument against you, with deadly results. The Remainers and probably yourself to a degree also wallowed in nostalgia for a time past, albeit of a more recent vintage. This was of cosy European summits when everyone hugged and kissed each other, travels in Tuscany, student exchange trips, wine tasting in Bordeaux, operas in Milan and fine, candlelit cuisine in Paris.'

Mike smiled and nodded in agreement, there were plenty of hard-hitting truths in what Eamon had said yet he felt for a moment he should fight back, give a counter argument. No, Costas had been right, if you can do something about it, do it. If not, don't bother. There was no point in fighting this fight. Or was there? Eamon finished his coffee and came around the table to shake his hand.

'Jane mentioned to me that you had an Irish father Michael, so you should be eligible to apply for an Irish passport. It might help you beat the queues at the airports.' He laughed, followed by Mike. 'Fortunately, you wouldn't be under any obligation to visit Ireland, thank God, all that rain, and the damned Irish would be enough to put you off for life.' They both laughed and hugged.

The descent began into Manchester. Where did he go from here? Jane was right, go back to the places of his formative years, see what had got under his skin the first time around, what made him so pro-European. Paris was already on the agenda and a reunion with Suzanne. There was so much old ground they would go over and Jane would be there too, the three of them laughing as Suzanne would tell Jane what an awful dancer he was, yet still managed to pick up the best-looking girl in the club. Next would be Pavel in Croatia and then take Jane to Sarajevo to see where the nightmare century started and finished. Maybe Vienna and Copenhagen and who knows, across the sea to the land of his fathers, perhaps with his Irish passport.

The three of them descended the staircase to retrieve their luggage from the carousel. He switched his phone back on and adjusted the time on his watch, ten minutes past midnight. He was tired and not looking forward to the drive home. The suitcases began to appear and feeling cold he zipped up his lightweight jacket. His phone rang, Jane looked at him and he shrugged. He looked at the display, it was Guy Simpson. What the hell did he want, at this time of night? He let it ring a couple of times hoping he would go away then answered.

'Guy, a bit late isn't it, even for you mate.'

'Mike, I'm so glad I've got you, I've been trying all evening. Listen, I've been asked to do a television series about what the Europeans think about Brexit. It's a big budget production Mike and I'm allowed to choose who I have with me. I want you, but I need a reply tonight. This is what I've got in mind. I take you and three other Brits out to Europe, two Remainers and two Brexiteers and we meet and greet politicians, business leaders and so on. You know the sort of crap I mean Mike, we'll have you and some senior bloke from BMW discussing the ramifications of Brexit over lunch in some picturesque setting with King Ludwig's castle in the background. The Brits will love it and we're working on a prime-time spot, hopefully Sunday night at nine. We'll start off in the four capital cities of the biggest countries left in the EU, France, Germany, Italy and Spain. What do you think mate, which city shall we go to first?'

Mike drew breath and said:

'Berlin.'

Lightning Source UK Ltd.
Milton Keynes UK
UKOW05f1733120717
PP1606500001B/1/P